MY ELF DADDY

MISTVALE SPIN-OFF

STELLA RAINBOW

Contents

Dedicated to:
Every person out there who defies the stereotypes on a daily basis. Keep being you, because you're awesome!

One

Westley

I tapped my fingers on the steering wheel as I drove. It was a nice day today, and the rain that usually haunted Mistvale seemed nowhere to be found. Even though I absolutely loved how much it rained here in Mistvale, it was nice to see the sun sometimes. I sang along with the song playing on the radio as I drove toward the railway station. It was a Disney song, and I made a note to switch the radio station before I arrived at my destination. The last thing I needed was to make a weird impression on my boss's colleague. Well, technically, Noel wasn't my boss. Rebba was. But while working for them, I'd realized that Rebba and Noel seemed to work in tandem, and though I knew Rebba was the owner of the animal shelter and even the farm—I think—Noel worked just as hard as her, and it didn't seem like either of them was higher up on the chain than the other.

Parking the car in the vacant lot of the railway station, I took a deep breath as I looked around. Mistvale itself didn't have a railway station of its own, just a bus stop that led to the other, bigger towns nearby. So, I'd had to drive down to the railway station, one town over, to pick up Noel's colleague, a man named Birch Sunday—who, I guessed by his name, was an old man, probably someone wrinkly and gray-haired. Wait. Why was I imagining Santa? I shook my head, rolling my eyes at the weird thoughts running through my mind.

I switched the radio over to the pop station and got out of the truck before locking it behind me. I straightened my clothes and made sure my badges and pins weren't sticking out too much as I made my way into the railway station. Just like the outside, the inside was empty of people, and I sighed in relief as I walked over to the board with the schedule on it. Mr. Sunday's train would arrive in less than a minute, so I headed to the platform and pushed my hands into my pockets as I waited.

A tap on my shoulder made me jerk, and I turned around to find myself face-to-face with the sexiest man I'd ever seen. The man was a few inches taller than me with dark brown hair pushed back on top of his head in a poof. Pointed ears framed his face, and I had the strange urge to run my fingertip over them to see if they were as sharp as they looked. His dark, almost black, eyes gazed at me with a look so intense that it made me shiver, and I just wanted to run my fingers through that sexy brown beard of his. He was maybe in his late thirties, and he was everything I ever looked for in a man. He was so my type.

My shoulders slumped as I remembered that even though he was exactly my type, I wasn't anyone's type. I wasn't a twink. I was chubby, but I wasn't muscular. I wasn't hairy enough to be a bear, but I also wasn't all smooth skin. I was everything a little shouldn't be. There was no way I could be anyone's type. Especially a daddy's. Not that this man was a daddy, though he did give off those daddy vibes.

The man snapped his fingers in front of my eyes, and I blinked as I realized I'd lost myself in my thoughts. I met the man's eyes, and he raised a brow at me questioningly. I shook my head before straightening up and giving him a smile.

"Are you Mr. Sunday?" I asked and the man nodded before giving me a once over. I shivered under his intense gaze but forced myself to not react further. The last thing I needed was for him to realize that I was remotely interested in him. I knew what happened when I showed interest. And I did not intend to make this man look at me with the same expression of disgust—or, even worse, pity—that I usually got from someone I tried to flirt with. I didn't want to watch him flounder as he tried to make up a reason for why he didn't want me. There was no reason to lie though, because I knew I wasn't the most good-looking man out there.

With my weight and the fact that I was a little, dating was just a dream for me, not something I could actually have in real life. Finding the perfect man who would also be my daddy? Pssh, that was only possible in my imagination. It wasn't like I'd never tried. The fact was that I'd tried too many times, but forcing scenes with Doms who didn't care about me in the least were the worst things *ever*. Even worse than that time I'd fallen asleep and somehow rolled over into Snuggles' poop. I'd been broken and thrown away way too many times and I was done. I could be little by myself, and my left hand was more than enough for me.

"Yeah, that's me," he said and I startled as I realized I'd lost myself in my thoughts. Again. I gave him a small smile before taking his luggage from his hand and waving him toward the exit. Mr. Sunday nodded before following me. We walked side by side to the car, and I opened the passenger side door for him.

His eyebrows rose a bit, but he moved into the seat as I put his luggage in the trunk before walking over to the driver's side.

I turned the radio on as I started the car, and the sound of guitars and other instruments filled the air, making me cringe. Pop wasn't my favorite genre, but it was what most people enjoyed. Personally, I was more of a theme song kind of guy, but I thought playing "Let It Go" wouldn't go over well with this man. Or with anyone, I guessed.

Rebba, Noel, and the others were almost used to my quirks by now. They didn't look at me weird when I walked around wearing overalls or my badges. They didn't care if I spent hours snuggling the bunnies in the mini shelter. As long as I did my work, they let me be and let me do whatever I wanted around the place. I'd been surprised when Noel had first offered me the job, but since he'd done it while I was being kicked out of my flat for being late on the payment, I hadn't been able to say no, and I was glad for it. Though I restricted most of my little tendencies to my home, I couldn't control myself when I was in the mini shelter. Those bunnies were just too cute, and every time I looked at them, it was like they were asking me to cuddle them, and how could I say no to those furry little faces, right?

Mr. Sunday leaned over to the dashboard and turned the volume down until the music was just a hum in the background, and I couldn't stop myself from smiling softly. It seemed like I wasn't the only one with an aversion to pop songs. The drive to Mistvale was quiet but not uncomfortable. I couldn't help sneaking glances at the man beside me every once in a while. He was just so good-looking! There was this aura about him, this assuredness that I was infinitely attracted to. He gave off this air of confidence that I was kind of familiar with. Back when I lived in a town where there were more than a few clubs, I'd went to a BDSM club a few times. I'd never managed to snag myself a daddy, obviously, but the vibe the other Doms gave off was exactly like the feeling I got from this man. I knew it was just wishful thinking on my part. My brain was trying to rope anyone and everyone into being my daddy.

I wasn't that lucky. My perfect daddy wouldn't just drop into my lap like this, now, would he? I shook off the fancy thoughts and focused on driving as I sneaked another glance at him, only to find him watching me. He raised a brow at me, and I flushed as I turned back to look out the windshield. Crap, I'd been caught.

The blush was still there when we arrived at the farmland. The farm was a Christmas tree farm, though there were a few cabins where Rebba, Noel, Caleb, and Devon lived. I'd managed to snag the tiny cabin that stood a few paces away from the mini shelter. It had come with the job, and it was probably my favorite part about it. Living in this place was heaven. I had all the privacy I needed, and there were a bunch of cute animals ready for cuddling just a few steps away from my house. What more could I ask for?

A daddy, my subconscious supplied, and I shook my head as I turned off the engine. *Keep dreaming, Wes,* I told myself. That was the only time I'd get to have a daddy, after all.

Birch

The boy who'd come to pick me up was interesting. I couldn't bring myself to call him a man, even though that was exactly what he was. He looked young, like he was in his late twenties, with round cheeks, a smiling face, and hazel eyes that seemed to suck me in. His eyes were bright and full of a quiet joy that made me want to fall deep into them. His colorful outfit and the quirky little badges he'd pinned to his T-shirt under his jacket brought out my daddy side. I didn't know if I should trust my instinct, but this boy screamed little to me.

But I couldn't be that lucky, could I? Yes, I was looking forward to moving here, at least I was thinking about it. When I'd picked up this project, my last as the CEO of The Easter branch at The Christmas, I hadn't expected much. The job itself was something my juniors were more than equipped to handle, but I'd heard a lot about the town of Mistvale, about how inclusive it was. I'd heard that many supes resided here, including the elf I was here to meet. While I'd hoped for a place to call home, I never expected it to feel so right. After spending the last six decades working for The Easter, I was looking forward to settling down somewhere. I'd hoped Mistvale would be that place, but until now I hadn't been sure.

Now that I had met this boy, I knew this had been a good decision. I also knew that Fate played a hand in me coming to Mistvale. It had to be her doing, right? I wasn't getting ahead of myself, was I? My instinct told me that Westley was someone special, someone who could be important to me. The sweet way he'd smiled at me when he'd been lost in thought had pulled something in my heart. It had touched a part of me that I hadn't had a chance to explore for a while now.

Sure, I'd had boys before. But none had seemed like they were the one. We would play, have a few nights of fun, but just that small interaction with Westley told me he'd be different. That was, if all my instincts about him were even correct. For all I knew, he was just a perpetually happy man.

Shaking my head to get rid of my fancy imagination, I glanced out the window at the town of Mistvale as Westley drove.

Mistvale was beautiful. Trees lined the streets, and though the sky looked blue today, the leaves were covered with a sheen of wetness as if it had rained just yesterday. Even though it was nearly spring, there was no sign of the rain letting up. I'd heard that Mistvale was prone to rain, but I hadn't realized the extent of it until now.

It looked as good a place as any to settle down, and if something really did happen between me and Westley, I knew I would be only too happy to stay.

Lord, I needed to stop imagining a future with this boy minutes after meeting him. If he could read my mind right now, I knew he would be freaked out. I wasn't usually like this. Hell, I couldn't even remember the last time I'd been interested in someone, much less so enamored that I'd started dreaming of a future with them minutes after meeting them. But my instinct, that place deep inside me where my magic resided, told me that this boy—this man—was important. Maybe it had been Fate's plan all along, bringing me here to this small town full of magic. Or maybe it had just been my luck. But whatever it was, I knew that this sweet boy was going to play a big role in my life henceforth.

I just hoped my instincts weren't wrong and that the sweet boy sitting beside me *was* a little.

Two

Westley

I stepped out of the car and spotted Aeron and Niall walking over to their car. I exchanged a waved with them, their eyes flitting toward Mr. Sunday and back before they got into their car and drove away. My cheeks were still flushed from getting caught staring at Mr. Sunday as I approached his side of the car. I opened his door to find him smirking up at me. I flushed even deeper and stepped back as he got out and closed the door behind him.

I grabbed his bags from the trunk and shuffled my feet as I wondered what I should do before realizing I should lead Mr. Sunday to Noel. After all, the two of them were colleagues, right? So that's what I was supposed to do. I waved Mr. Sunday toward the clearing where all our cabins were and followed a step behind him. Why hadn't Noel told me what to do once I had brought him home? I hated not knowing what I was supposed to do. It was so much better when someone told me exactly what I needed to do. It was so much easier. If Mr.

Sunday was my daddy, I would have asked him what I was supposed to do.

Freezing at the thought that had crossed my mind, I shook myself before I resumed walking. I needed to stop thinking like that. Needed to stop staring at Mr. Sunday as he walked a step in front of me. I needed to stop thinking that he might mean something to me when it was absolutely impossible.

Wasn't it enough that I was big and chubby and *little*? Why couldn't I be attracted to the big, muscular types who could at least let me sit on their lap without getting crushed? Why did I have to be attracted to leaner, smaller guys? Guys like Birch. *Mr. Sunday*, I corrected myself. Why couldn't I just be attracted to guys who could be my daddy instead of wanting men like Birch who wouldn't even give me a second glance? And why would he? He was gorgeous. He could get any guy—or girl—he wanted. Why would he ever want someone like me? I wasn't even all that good-looking.

I rubbed my finger on one of my badges in order to clear my thoughts. I knew that thinking badly about myself wouldn't do me any good. And if I had a daddy, he would punish me for it. Not that that was looking possible anytime in the future. Still, the fuzzy velvet of my badge comforted me a bit, and I was almost back to myself by the time we reached the clearing, where Noel and his friends were still cleaning up after one of Noel's usual dinner nights. Gus and Cassian walked around putting away chairs, and Noel was wiping down a table. He started to call something out to Gus when he spotted me and Mr. Sunday. Noel walked toward us, a smile spreading across his lips, his dark curls bouncing merrily. I loved how happy he always was. It was like having a younger brother when I talked to him. Like having someone who cared. I returned his smile as he drew close.

He extended his hand toward Mr. Sunday. "Hey, you must be Birch. I'm Noel, and my mate Caleb is somewhere around here. I hope your trip was okay."

I'd found it curious the first time Noel had called Caleb his mate. But then Noel had explained that Jai, one of his friends, had discovered the word mate in one of his romance books, and they'd all loved it so much that they'd taken to calling their boyfriends their mates. It was kinda cute, to be honest.

Mr. Sunday nodded his head as he shook hands with Noel, giving him a small smile. "The trip was okay. The drive here was perfect."

I looked at him to find him watching me, and I blushed again before looking away, only to meet Noel's eyes. He raised his brow at me, his expression curious, and I shook my head before looking away again. Shit. The last thing I needed was one of my friends to get a whiff of my thoughts. They were all amazing, but they could be a bit meddlesome. I was glad they hadn't discovered my little side yet. I knew they wouldn't treat me badly because of it. I just feared they would get too involved. That was the kind of people they were, after all. But I still loved them. They were my family now.

"Westley, why don't you show Birch to his cabin while I finish with the cleanup. I'll send some dinner to your room, Birch. How about you relax for tonight and we can talk tomorrow?" Noel asked, turning toward Mr. Sunday. Mr. Sunday nodded before glancing at me again, and I wondered why he was staring at me. Had I done something? Made him uncomfortable somehow? Or was he just repaying me for all the staring I did in the car?

Whatever it was, he was still staring at me. And when he watched me with that intense look in his eyes, it made me feel . . . special. Like I was someone important.

"Yeah, tomorrow sounds good. I'd love to take a shower and relax."

"Westley, why don't you show Birch to the cabin near my place? I'll send some dinner in a few, alright?"

"Sure, Noel. Do you need any help with cleaning up? I can come back after I drop Mr. Sunday off?"

"No, we are fine. After you're done, go on to your cabin. I'll get some dinner for you too. I don't need you working yourself to the bone, alright? You're my best employee, and a great friend. I don't want to make you sick or anything."

I shook my head, smiling at Noel, knowing he wouldn't let me work more today. It was just as well. I was feeling a bit tired.

"Alright. See you tomorrow, then."

Noel waved us off, and I led Mr. Sunday toward Noel's cabin or more precisely to the guest cabin beside his.

Birch

I slept fitfully, my dreams filled with a round-cheeked boy sitting on my lap as I read stories to him. His hazel eyes watched me with such adoration that my heart ached when I woke up with empty arms. What the hell was happening to me? I'd met the boy just yesterday. Surely, I couldn't be so enamored by him in such a short time? We had barely talked for fuck's sake. How could it be that someone I'd had a single conversation with was starring in my dreams all of a sudden? How could one meeting with this sweet little boy affect me so thoroughly?

I dragged my fingers through my hair as I closed my eyes, his picture immediately forming behind my eyelids. His cheeks were rosy with a blush, and he was dressed in an outfit I'd picked out for him. A fuzzy bunny suit that had a hood with ears and a small fluffy tail. He looked adorable with his short hair sticking out of the hoodie and his hands covered in fluffy gloves. He was a cute little bunny. My bunny. Seemed apt for Easter, didn't it?

I shook my head and opened my eyes. Imagining things about the sweet boy would bring me nothing but pain when I realized that he wasn't the one for me. I knew nothing about him. Was he even into men? And if by some miracle he was, what were the chances he was little, too? I had zero clue about him, and I needed to change that because I felt a connection with him. Like most supes, elves had mates too. But unlike most supes, we couldn't sense our mates. Noel had been lucky in the fact that his mate was a wolf shifter, and shifters could scent their mates. I'd spent years wondering if I'd already met my mate and just hadn't recognized him, but now I felt like maybe I'd been wrong. Could it really be him? Could Westley be my mate? Could my coming here be something Fate had already decided would happen?

I straightened as determination coursed through me. I would get to know Westley first and then let my instinct decide what to do. Maybe I would discover he already had a girlfriend or a boyfriend, and I would know to step back. Or maybe, just maybe, I'd finally find what I had been looking for for the past few decades.

I took a shower even though I'd showered before bed last night and brushed my teeth before dressing up in my usual attire of a white dress shirt and a pair of suit pants. This set was a dark brown color that matched my hair, or so my cousin had said. I combed my hair before taking a deep breath and walking out of the cabin.

It was only when I was outside that I realized I'd woken up way too early. The clearing was empty save for a bobcat that stalked through the trees. I remembered Noel telling me that one of the pack members was a bobcat and I figured it was him. I shook my head as I wondered where I should go. I walked around the clearing and just looked at the place. After all, that was part of my project, wasn't it?

The project I'd used as an excuse to come here was to host an Easter party of sorts. The Easter was thinking of branching out into hosting Easter parties for kids, and we decided to do a trial run this year at Noel's place. After all, the pack land was owned by our company, so it was the most likely place for it, and Noel had been excited when he was told of the plan, so it worked out pretty well for everyone involved. Originally, the plan had been for one of the juniors to lead this project, but when I heard about the town, I decided to do it myself. They knew I was retiring soon, so they hadn't created much of a fuss when I'd asked to be the head of this project. It didn't require much work, but it included a visit to Mistvale, so I'd been all into it. I looked up as I reached a building that didn't look like the other cabins. This building was bigger and felt different.

I moved closer and tried to listen and figure out what it was. A bark sounded from inside, followed by a soft meow, and I realized this was the mini shelter Noel had been talking about. I wanted to check out the shelter, or "The Happy Place" as Noel had called it, but it was on the other side of the town. So, I decided to peek into the mini shelter and figure out what kind of animals were inside. I tried to turn the knob and realized it was open. Obviously, they had no reason to lock animals in when the place was full of shifters who would realize the moment one escaped.

I stepped into the room and was surprised to hear a familiar voice coming from the room down the hallway. I quickened my steps but made sure not to make much noise. I wasn't sure why I was sneaking but I was.

I slid the door open softly and stuck my head in to see what Westley was up to. What I saw made all the doubts rush out of my head and forced everything to fall into place. I had no doubts now. Westley was my boy. Westley had been meant for me and he would be my boy, my little boy.

Three

Westley

I rolled over onto my back, pulling Snuggles closer to me as I cuddled him. From the three bunnies the mini shelter held, Snuggles was my favorite. Cookie and Sleepy were still asleep in their cage, but Snuggles was always up for some cuddle time with me.

I rubbed his ear between my thumb and index finger as I let his fluffy goodness comfort me. This was a tradition of ours. Every morning, before all the others woke up, I sneaked into the mini shelter and had a cuddle session with my bunnies. They weren't exactly *my* bunnies, but if I didn't have to work all day, I would have definitely adopted them. Either way, spending the morning with them centered me and made it easier for me to tackle a full work day.

Being in my little space for a while gave me the strength to go through the day without letting my anxiety or stress get the best of me. But today, I couldn't quite get into the proper mindset. My mind was full of intense dark eyes watching me as I cuddled Snuggles. The thoughts stopped me from sinking into my little space completely, and I teetered somewhere on the edge. Not quite into my little space, but not feeling all that big either. I wanted him. Wanted him to be taking care of me, to be here with me while I played with my bunnies.

"Snuggles, I wish he was mine. I wish he could be my daddy. I mean, I don't even know if he's into men, much less if he's into daddy kink. And even if by some stupid miracle he is, why would he ever want me?" I murmured, my voice a bit higher pitched than usual, telling me I was much closer to my little side than I'd thought. But I still couldn't quite sink into it completely. I pulled Snuggles closer to me, running my fingers through his soft, silky fur. "I wish . . . I wish I could have him, Snuggles. Ever since I saw him yesterday, he's all I've been able to think about. I need to stop daydreaming, right? He isn't for me. No one is for me."

I sighed as I closed my eyes, urging myself to let go of this fantasy I'd made up. Mr. Sunday was so out of my league it wasn't even funny. There was no way he could be interested in me. I needed to get that through my stupid heart because it was starting to hope and hope only ever led to heartbreak. I didn't want to get my heart broken.

Rolling to my side, I placed Snuggles beside me on the mat we were laying on before opening my eyes. They widened as they fell on the figure standing in the doorway. I froze when I spotted Mr. Sunday just leaning against the doorway like he hadn't just witnessed me embarrassing myself. Crap. How long had he been standing there? Had he heard everything? Had he realized I was talking about him? I scrambled to my feet, grabbing Snuggles and pulling him to me as I swiftly walked over to his cage and put him inside. After giving all three of the bunnies gentle head pats, I turned around to find Mr. Sunday still watching me, his dark eyes as intense as always.

I shivered under his gaze, but didn't meet his eyes, preferring to look anywhere but at him.

What did I do? Did I talk to him or did I just leave? I had no clue what I would say if I could even bring myself to talk in the first place. I lowered my head, mumbling something about getting to work, and before he could stop me, I rushed out of the room. I knew that if he said even one word, if he told me to stop, I would. I would stop without a second thought, but he didn't stop me. He let me go, and for some reason, that hurt. At least it told me that I'd been right. He didn't want me, not like I wanted him. If he'd wanted me, surely he would have stopped me, right? He would have asked questions, asked me what I was talking about. Maybe he had heard everything, and he was weirded out by me.

I stumbled to a stop at the door to my cabin as realization struck. What if he told Noel about it? What if he told Noel that I was a freak and a pervert? What if Noel believed him and kicked me out? What would I do then? This was the first time in a long while that I'd found a place where I felt like I could belong. I felt like this place could be my home. I didn't want to leave. But if Mr. Sunday told them about me, they would make me leave. Right? And I would be right back where I used to be. On the outside, looking in at all the friends and family that I'd always wanted but would never have. I didn't want that. I couldn't bear to be alone again.

I walked into my house and promptly threw myself on the couch, burying my face in the pillows. I whimpered softly as I squeezed my eyes shut to keep the tears at bay. I prayed to God Mr. Sunday would keep it to himself, that he wouldn't tell the others. Maybe if I begged him not to, if I told him I'd do anything he told me to, he would keep my secret. Maybe he wouldn't say anything anyway. Maybe he was a good guy, and I just needed to give him a chance.

After I'd calmed myself a bit, I sat up and took a deep breath. I needed to get to work. I didn't want to give anyone another reason to kick me out. And whatever happened with Mr. Sunday, I would deal with it. Just like I'd dealt with everything life threw at me before. Everything would be okay. Right?

Not for the first time, I wished I had a daddy who would hold me in his arms and tell me everything would be okay.

Birch

I watched my boy as he rushed outside, mumbling something about getting to work. I thought about going after him but realized that I wanted to do this right. I needed to give him some space. It was clear he was embarrassed by getting caught, and I wanted to show him that it was okay. That what he wanted was completely okay, and that I would be more than happy to give it to him. I'd heard him tell the bunny about wanting someone he had met yesterday. It could only be me, right? I wasn't alone in this fascination I had with the boy. We had a connection. And I planned on exploring it. Decision made, I walked out of the mini shelter and spotted Westley rushing into his cabin. Was he okay? I considered going and checking on him, but my instinct told me he needed a moment alone, so I trusted it. I needed a plan anyway, so it was only right to let him have a moment while I figured out what I would do next.

After spending quite a few minutes watching Westley's front door as I debated with myself, I decided to walk over to Noel's cabin. Soft sounds coming from the inside told me he was still home, so I rapped my knuckles on the door and waited for him to open it. The door was opened a moment later by a bulky man with brown hair and cool gray-blue eyes that scanned me from head to toe, as if looking for a threat. It took me a moment to figure out that he was Noel's mate.

"Caleb, right?" I asked and he nodded before shifting away to let me in.

"I'm guessing you are Birch Sunday," he said and I returned the nod as I shook his outstretched hand before taking the seat he offered me on the couch. Noel stepped out of the kitchen a moment later with a tray in his hand and smiled when he spotted me.

"Birch! I was just about to come over to invite you for breakfast. I hope pancakes are okay," he said and his cheerfulness had me smiling too.

"Yeah, it's more than okay. You didn't have to go to the trouble of it, though." Even as I said it, my stomach growled softly and Caleb smirked at me, telling me he'd heard it with his canine hearing. I shrugged before turning to the delicious looking pancakes Noel was offering me on a plate.

"Shush. I wanted to make you breakfast." He handed me the plate, and I breathed in the delicious scent of blueberry pancakes.

"So, Noel said you are planning to host an Easter party here?" Caleb asked and I nodded as I chewed, biting back a moan at the delicious taste.

I hurried to swallow before saying, "Yes. It's my last project as the CEO and I'm excited about it."

"CEO? This party doesn't sound like something that would fall under a CEO's job, to be honest." Caleb said, a curious lilt to his voice and I smiled.

"It isn't. This was supposed to be my junior's project, but when I heard he was coming to Mistvale, I decided to take it up myself."

"Oh, you wanted to visit Mistvale, you mean?" Noel asked as I stabbed another bite of delicious pancake.

"Yeah, I'm thinking about moving here, actually. I've been the CEO of The Easter branch for a while now, and I'm planning to settle down. So, when I heard about Mistvale, about how inclusive it was, I decided to check it out and see if it might be the place."

"Mistvale is pretty awesome. Have you decided yet or are you wanting to see more of it? I can tell you about all the places you could check out if you want," Noel said, a twinkle in his eyes told me he knew more than he was revealing.

I smiled as I thought about the cute boy who had run to his cabin just minutes ago and replied, "I'm staying. I like what I've seen of Mistvale so far, and I think this is the place for me."

"Oh, I bet it is." Noel smirked and Caleb gave him a raised brow, telling me Noel knew exactly why I wanted to stay here.

I smiled at him and shrugged my shoulders, answering his question without really saying anything.

"Westley is family to me, alright?" Noel said. And even though he was anything but threatening, I took his warning seriously. He may be a tiny little thing, but I knew that if I did anything to hurt his family, I would be in big trouble.

Caleb gave Noel a confused look before turning to me. Realization dawned in his eyes as he looked between us, and he smirked before turning serious and facing me again. "Yeah, Westley is family now, so you better be careful." Caleb was much more threatening than his mate, and I raised my palms up in a placating gesture. I would take care of my boy. Westley would soon be my responsibility, and I planned on being the best daddy ever.

"I'll take care of him." I promised. Noel smiled at me while Caleb nodded approvingly. We continued with breakfast as I planned a date with Westley in my mind. First things first though, I needed to ask him out and show him that we wanted the exact same thing.

After breakfast, Noel and I discussed the ins and outs of the party, who we would invite, and what activities we would include. It wasn't a long discussion since this really was supposed to be a small project, but somehow, we kept skipping from one topic to the next, and three hours later, I was *finally* free to go. I needed to go out, look around the town, and figure out what Westley and I would be doing for our date. I wanted to show him we could be good together, that we had a connection. And I also wanted to tell him that I understood what he wanted. That I wanted it too. And for that, I needed to get to work. I had a plan. Now, all I needed to do was put it into action. Not having Westley was not an option, and I needed to do my best to make him see that we were meant to be together.

Four

Westley

I sat on my couch with my arms wrapped around me as I wondered what I should do. I hadn't seen Mr. Sunday anywhere all day after our early morning encounter. I didn't know where he was, just that he wasn't on the farm grounds. Honestly, I was a bit relieved that he wasn't here. I had no clue what I would say to him when I met him, and the anxiety was biting away at me, making me restless and unsettled. I chewed the nail of my thumb as I rocked softly, trying to figure out if I should go talk to him.

What would I say? What would I tell him about what he had overheard this morning? Could I tell him the truth, or would he think I was a sicko, a freak? I knew not everyone understood kink, especially things like daddy and little relationships. I hadn't explored much, hadn't had the chance to with the kind of life I'd lived until I came here. I'd had a few scenes in a club before, but they hadn't been all that fun. It was difficult to let go of your worries and let a stranger care for you. Despite that, I knew what I wanted. Even if I didn't have much experience. But I also knew that kink was something a lot of people misunderstood. The last thing I wanted was for my new friends to be disgusted by me or think badly of me. I wouldn't be able to deal with it if I had to leave this place.

A big part of me wanted to just ignore everything. Ignore Mr. Sunday, ignore the fact that he had caught me pretty much red-handed. But there were a lot of what-ifs. And I couldn't live with the uncertainty and anxiety either.

Before I could come to a decision, a knock on my door jerked me out of my thoughts. I'd locked the door for the night, figuring I would try to relax before making a quick dinner for myself and going to bed. Who could it be? I glanced at the clock and realized it was almost seven in the evening. Working at the farm meant my workday ended by six at the latest. I'd planned on having a bit of playtime with my stuffed toys and coloring books to get my mind off what had happened this morning. But it seemed like I was needed at work. I shrugged as I got to my feet, running my palms down my front to make sure I was presentable. I hadn't changed into my jammies yet, so I was still wearing a normal, adult-ish outfit. Thank goodness for comfy T-shirts and gray sweatpants.

I opened the door and my stomach dropped when I found Mr. Sunday on the other side with his hands behind his back. I grew a little dizzy as I met that same intense gaze that had me shivering every time he looked my way since the train station.

"Mr. Sunday? What can I do for you?" I asked, as if he hadn't just caught me talking to my bunnies this morning about making him my daddy.

Mr. Sunday raised his brow at me and said, "Call me Birch, okay?"

I nodded mutely before stepping away and letting him into the house. I could see that he was hiding something behind his back, but he made sure I couldn't see it as he walked into the room and took a seat on the couch. This piqued my little side's interest, and I sneaked closer to him, though I didn't sit down. I stood in front of him, shuffling my feet as I tried to figure out what to say. "Mr. Su—Birch, about this morning. I'm really sorry about what you saw. I really didn't mean anything by it, please don't tell anyo—"

"Stop." My teeth clacked together. That was how fast I shut my mouth at that stern voice of his. God, that was such a daddy tone he had used. I couldn't stop the shudder from racking through me as my eyes drifted close for just a second.

"Come, sit here," Birch said and my eyes snapped open as I saw that he was patting the couch beside him. I eyed him warily before taking a seat, wincing when the couch sank a bit beneath my weight. The cabin hadn't been furnished when I'd moved here, and I'd saved up to get this couch from a garage sale. It was clear it wasn't new, and beneath my weight, it had already started to sink in. I hoped Birch wouldn't notice the dip as I wrapped my arms around myself and turned to face him.

"Westley, I wanted to ask you something," Birch said and I nodded to show I was listening.

He finally brought his hand out from behind him and offered me a paper bag. I couldn't quite stop myself from taking the bag and peeking into it curiously. My eyes widened when I spotted the brown fur, and I pulled the stuffie out as a smile spread across my lips. It was a bunny. But the best thing was the bunny looked exactly like Snuggles. It was brown all over with a white spot on its nose and the backs of its ears. It was as if someone had taken a picture of Snuggles and turned it into a stuffed bunny.

"This is for me?" I asked, my voice ringing with glee as I looked up at him. Birch smiled softly at me and his smile was so beautiful. In the time since I'd met him, he hadn't smiled once, not like this anyway. His lips were tilted upwards in a gentle curve, and I knew without doubt that it was an expression only a few people got to see. And it seemed like I was one of them.

"Do you like it?" he asked and I could barely hear the strain of nerves in his voice as he spoke.

I nodded swiftly and hugged the bunny close to my chest, loving the way its soft fur rubbed against the base of my throat.

"I love it. Thank you so much." It was only once I'd calmed down a little bit that I realized what this meant. At least what I hoped it meant. "So, you don't mind? You don't think I am a sicko? A freak?" I asked, my voice barely a whisper.

That intense look was back in Birch's eyes as he shook his head. "You're none of that, Westley. You're sweet, adorable, and I want you to be my boy."

"What?" I asked, my jaw dropping to the floor. I hadn't expected that. Was he making fun of me? He wouldn't be that mean, would he?

"Are you being mean?" I asked and I could hear the slight whimper in my voice. I hadn't meant to sound as childish, as *little* as I did, but I didn't know what else to say. It was all so confusing.

"Westley, I'm not joking. I like you. Granted, I don't know much about you, but I feel this connection with you. This draw. And I would like to explore it if you are interested too. Will you go out with me? On a date?"

He wasn't joking. I could see the honest interest in his eyes, in the way his palm wrapped softly over the back of my hand. He really wanted this. Wanted me. Was I dreaming? That had to be it, right? No way did this gorgeous, sexy man want me.

"You're a daddy?" I asked, just to make sure we were on the same page.

Birch nodded, the smile still on his lips as his hand came up and he ran a finger down my cheek. "Yes, my sweet boy. And I'd like nothing more than to have you as my boy, as my little bunny. Only if you want it too, of course. Want me."

"I want you!" I answered a bit too enthusiastically and Birch laughed, a warm loud sound that sent shivers down my spine.

"So? Will you go out on a date with me tomorrow night?" he asked and I nodded instantly, a wide smile spreading across my lips to match his. Last night, I had been dreaming of this moment, and now it had actually happened. Could a boy get any luckier?

Birch

He'd said yes! After overhearing him earlier that morning, I had been hoping he would say yes. But I still hadn't completely expected it.

Dating had always been a touch difficult for me. Hell, I couldn't remember the last time I'd had a boy, though I knew it had been at least two decades. Or longer. The thing was, I wasn't the typical daddy material. For one, I was short. I was still taller than Westley, but I wasn't as big as daddies usually were. The fact that most daddies were silver foxes, or at least had salt-and-pepper hair, was another thing that made me different. I was lean, not buff or cuddly like the daddies at the club usually were. All my previous boyfriends had liked me as a person, but they'd always found me lacking as a daddy. And yet, being a daddy was such an important part of me that I couldn't fully commit to a relationship without it.

Despite all the failed attempts, here I was, taking a chance again. But something about Westley told me he would be different. Maybe it was the fact that he wasn't the typical boy either. He was big, cuddly, and I couldn't wait to wrap my arms around him and hold him all night long.

I looked around the room, finally taking a moment to look at my boy's house. The decor was sparse, but everything he owned looked clean and well taken care of. It was clear he treasured his home.

"Have you had dinner yet?" I asked and Westley shook his head, his eyes still a little too wide for his face.

"I-I was just about to make it. Would you like to stay for dinner?" he asked and then his cheeks darkened immediately, as if he'd just realized what he'd said. "I mean, you don't have to. I know our date is tomorrow. I'm not trying to hurry you."

I chuckled softly, loving the flustered blush on his cheeks. "I would love to stay for dinner. But, tell you what? Why don't I make something for us while you get dressed in something more comfortable?" I asked, something telling me that the T-shirt and sweatpants he wore weren't his usual nighttime attire. Call it an instinct, or my daddy side directing me, but I just knew.

"Should I? I'm not uncomfortable in these clothes. I don't need to change," he said but it seemed like he was trying to convince himself instead of me. I just raised my brow at him, letting him see that I wasn't buying it. After a moment, he sighed before showing me to the kitchen.

"There isn't a lot of stuff in here. Noel usually invites me over for dinner most days. But you might find stuff for some sandwiches or something, I think." Westley seemed embarrassed at the lack of food in his refrigerator, but I didn't really care. If this worked out, if I became his daddy, I would make sure he always had something to eat. But right now, he was doing the best he could, and I was proud of him for that.

"Don't worry, I'll figure something out. Go on and get changed," I insisted and he huffed before walking over to the other room, which was obviously his bedroom. It seemed like my boy would have a bratty side when he fully came into his little side, and I couldn't wait to see it. I busied myself looking through the contents of the refrigerator and decided on a simple chicken sandwich to go with the bottle of orange juice I'd found. I was glad to see that there was no alcohol in his refrigerator, not even a beer. Not that I had any problem with people who drank alcohol, but I wanted my boy to be the healthiest he could, and alcohol didn't always help with that.

By the time I got the sandwiches ready and juice poured into glasses, Westley still hadn't come out of his room. I hadn't found any special plates in his cabinets, so I'd gone with traditional cutlery, making a mental note to ask more about what age Westley regressed to once I had a chance.

Placing the food and drinks on the coffee table, I walked over to the closed bedroom door and knocked softly. "Westley? Are you done?"

"Just a minute." His voice was soft, and he sounded slightly nervous. Was he scared of showing me his comfy clothes? Only a moment later, the door snicked and I stepped back as it opened. A smile spread across my lips as the vision from my dreams came true. Westley stood on the other side of the doorway, dressed in a gray onesie that looked velvety soft and reminded me of a bunny. My bunny. He looked absolutely adorable as he fidgeted with the hem of the sleeve, rubbing the soft fuzzy cloth between his thumb and index finger as he avoided meeting my eyes.

"You look absolutely adorable, my sweet boy," I assured and he looked up at me, his eyes hopeful.

"I do?" he asked and I nodded as I raised my hand up to run my fingers through his short hair. He leaned into my touch immediately, as if he'd been starving for it, and I made a note to touch him as much as I could. I never wanted him to want for anything, especially not my touch.

"You look like the most adorable little bunny ever. Come on, let's have some dinner," I said, watching his eyes and nose crinkle in pleasure. He walked over to the couch with me. I patted the space beside me and he settled immediately. I handed him his plate and waved at him to eat. As we ate, I made a mental list of all the things I needed to get for my boy. We hadn't decided on anything, yet in my mind, he was already my boy. I needed to get him some special plates, a sippy cup, and maybe some more cute little clothes. I wondered what he thought about diapers, but decided that was a conversation for a later date. It had been so long since I'd had a boy, but everything was coming back to me like it had been just under the surface, waiting for me to find my perfect boy. I knew exactly what I needed to do to make sure my boy was well taken care of, and I would be damned if I didn't take the best care of my little bunny.

Once we finished eating, Westley washed up the dishes despite my insistence that I could help him. When he was done, we stood in the living room, him fidgeting with the cuff of his onesie again while I tried to say goodnight. The last thing I wanted was to leave him. I wanted to stay, wanted to hold him in my arms all night long. But we'd just met, and despite the connection we shared, we were still practically strangers. We needed to get to know each other before we could do anything more.

"Alright, Westley. I'll see you tomorrow, okay? Can I pick you up around six?" I asked and Westley looked up at me, a small smile flitting across his plush lips. He nodded and shifted just a bit closer. I mirrored his movement until we were almost nose to nose and smiled.

"Before I go . . . I know this is more of an after-the-first-date thing, but I really want to kiss you. Can I kiss you, Westley?" I asked and his cheeks turned pink as his eyes fell to my lips. It took him a moment to return his gaze to mine, and when he did, his blush darkened even further. But he nodded and that was all I needed before I was pressing my lips to his. I didn't deepen the kiss, didn't try to taste his mouth, even though I desperately wanted to. I kept the kiss chaste, just pressing my lips to his soft, plush ones. The kiss was sweet and full of hope and anticipation. It was beautiful.

When I pulled back, my tongue sneaked out to taste my lips in an attempt to catch the slightest taste of him. My lips were sweet, with a hint of orange juice and a deeper sweetness that I could only attribute to Westley. My boy was sweet all over, and I couldn't wait to taste more of him.

"I'll see you tomorrow, Westley. Sweet dreams." I leaned forward and pressed a chaste kiss against his nose before turning around and walking over to the door. "Please close the door behind me, Westley. I want you to be safe, alright?"

"Yes, Da—Birch." Westley answered and my step stuttered as I realized he'd been about to say daddy. My heart warmed in my chest and a wide smile spread across my lips as I opened the front door and stepped outside. I closed the door behind me and leaned against it for a moment, relishing the warmth that was spreading through me, the hope and excitement for what was to come. I felt a connection with Westley, and I hoped it meant what I thought it did. But either way, I was looking forward to our date night, and I planned on making it the best date the boy had ever had.

Five

Westley

I glanced at myself in the mirror, hoping my outfit wasn't too out there. I wore a bright red T-shirt and my best pair of denim overalls. I'd fastened two of my favorite badges to the right shoulder strap. One pin was a bunny, the enamel a bright red color to match my T-shirt. The other was a peach with "I'm peachy" written across it. The pins were cute as hell, and they made my outfit perfect. They were just another way I let small parts of my little side sneak into my daily routine, and they made me feel like I was being true to myself. I slid on my rainbow-colored sneakers and took one last look at myself. I hoped Birch would like the way I dressed. He'd already seen me in overalls, so it wasn't like I would be surprising him with it.

I cracked my knuckles as I glanced at the clock and realized Birch would be here any minute. I was nervous. Very, very nervous. I'd never imagined this could happen, that Birch would actually want to date me. I didn't know how it had happened, or why Birch found me attractive. But he had asked me out and

I'd said yes. I just hoped I wouldn't make a mess of myself on this date of ours. I wanted him to like me, and I wanted him. I wanted him to be my daddy.

A knock on the door had me jumping out of my skin. He was here. I took a deep breath and walked over to the front door. I stood there for a second to steady myself before opening it.

God, Birch was gorgeous. His dark brown hair was slicked back, his beard begging for my fingers to scratch through it. His eyes were as dark as ever as they took me in, and I shivered under his intense gaze. He was dressed in a casual outfit, a navy-blue jacket thrown over a white T-shirt with dark jeans that clung to his legs like a second skin. He was so much leaner than me, and the fact attracted me to him immensely. He wasn't like any other daddy I had ever seen, and I loved it.

"Can I kiss you, Westley?" he asked and my heart skipped a beat in my chest as heat rushed up to my cheeks. With just a few words, he'd made almost all of my anxiety disappear. If he wasn't into me, surely he wouldn't be asking if he could kiss me, right? That meant he really wanted this, wanted me.

I stepped closer to him and pressed my lips to his, sighing against his lips as the nerves disappeared. This felt right, me and him. I didn't believe in fate or destiny, but me and Birch? We felt right, righter than anything I'd ever felt before.

As we kissed, his hands wrapped gently around my wrists, but all too soon, he was pulling away and offering me a brilliant smile. His palms rubbed over my arms as he spoke, "Are you ready?"

I nodded and closed the door behind me. I didn't need to lock it since there was no way anyone would try to sneak in. I followed Birch to the parking area and realized we were taking Noel's car. Birch opened the passenger side door for me, and

I stepped inside and settled into my seat, relishing the small gesture that was such a daddy thing to do. It looked like he had taken some time to acquaint himself with the town because he didn't seem the least bit hesitant driving down the road that led into the town.

"What kind of music do you like?" Birch asked. I flushed, wondering if he would like the answer I had or not.

He glanced at me out of the corner of his eye before turning back to look out the windshield. "Personally, I don't really have many favorites. I like some Christmas music, but otherwise most songs these days are just too . . . loud for my tastes, I guess."

I peeked over at him, surprised that he felt the same. "I . . . I like theme songs, you know, from movies and stuff." That was as far as I was ready to go right now. No way was I going to tell him that the movies I was talking about were Disney's.

"Oh yes, right. I especially love some of the songs from the kids' shows. Sometimes, they have much more meaning than the songs you hear these days." he confessed and I was pretty sure he heard the gasp I let out at that. I scanned his face to find him smiling softly, but he didn't turn to meet my eyes. Did he really mean that? Was he saying that just so I wouldn't be embarrassed? Either way, I loved it. I loved that he wanted to make me feel comfortable. I loved that he didn't mock my love for theme songs.

"Have you . . . have you been a daddy for long?" I asked and Birch shot me a smile. He squeezed my hand and I soaked in the feeling of his warm, smooth palm over mine.

"Yeah, I knew I was a daddy pretty early. I've had a few boys, but no one in the past few years. What about you? I'm guessing you are a little, but we didn't really talk about it."

I nodded, then realized he wasn't looking at me, so I spoke up, "Yes, I'm a little. I don't really have any experience to speak of. I've never had a daddy before. But I know what I want. It's just . . . I never really had a chance to experience it firsthand. If you haven't guessed it yet, I'm not the kind of boy most daddies look for or want." I hadn't meant to say it like that, like I didn't like myself. I did. I didn't hate myself. I liked that I was a bit bigger than most people. I liked thinking of myself as a cuddly bear. As someone sweet and gentle and loving. But, unfortunately, most people didn't think like that. And I guess over time, I'd let their opinions of me overshadow my own. I'd let their opinions turn me bitter against myself.

"Well, I think it was my good luck that you hadn't been snatched up already because you're exactly my type." Birch's voice was firm, full of sincerity, and it warmed my heart. I didn't know how I could be his type, but I was glad I was. Because he was definitely my type.

"You're my type, too," I admitted and his smile widened, which made me happy because that was all I wanted. To make him happy. To make my daddy happy. I didn't know where he was taking me, what his plan for our first date was. But I did know that I was already enjoying this more than I'd ever enjoyed a date. And this was just the beginning.

Birch

When we reached the park, I didn't waste a moment before getting out of the car and walking over to Westley's side to open his door. He seemed surprised when I did it, and I wondered how many times he'd had someone open the door for him before. From his reaction, I had to guess very few. But that changed now because I was here to take care of my boy, and it would be my pleasure to open all the doors for him. He gave me a sweet, wide eyed look as I offered him my hand, his cheeks turning pink, and my heart warmed as he took it instantly before climbing out of the car.

The park didn't look too crowded. Only a few older kids hung out near the fountain at the back while the rest of the park was empty. Coming here this late had been a good idea. The sky wasn't too cloudy, and it looked like the sun would stay for another hour. That would be perfect. Just enough time for us to have our picnic. Afterward, maybe we could take a nice walk down to the docks before heading home.

I'd decided to keep our first date a bit low-key. Mostly because I wasn't familiar enough with the town yet to know where the best places to hang out were. I also wanted to take Westley somewhere he could have fun. The park had seemed like a good idea. I looked over at Westley to find him smiling and bouncing on the balls of his feet as he looked around the park. Perfect.

"How is it that I've lived in this town for a few months now and still haven't been here before?" Westley asked, shaking his head in wonder.

"I thought we could have a picnic. Does that sound good?" I asked and Westley nodded immediately, clapping his hands.

"That sounds wonderful!"

Humming, I walked over to the trunk and brought out the basket Noel had helped me pack. The man was a lifesaver. He hadn't just helped me figure out where to take Westley on this date, he'd also helped me pack some food for the two of us. He seemed to know all of Westley's favorites, and I was glad I'd taken his help in packing. I also grabbed the blanket he'd given me, a colorful handwoven thing that I really didn't want to damage by sitting on it. Westley took the blanket from me, then took my free hand with a smile. I could've carried everything while holding his hand, but he seemed happy to hold the blanket, so I let him.

We walked over to a sunny patch of land. Well, as sunny as it ever got in Mistvale.

Westley spread the blanket for us and I sat down, pulling him with me. He stuck close to my side, not quite touching me, but still close enough that I could feel the warmth of his body. I shifted slightly so I was facing him, and he smiled as he looked around the place. His eyes snagged on the swing set, but then he shook his head and looked away. I knew exactly what had been going through his mind. Somehow, in the short time I'd known him, I'd started to understand him. Or maybe it was just the fact that I was a daddy and he was a little that helped me figure out where his mind had gone.

"You want to play on the swings for a bit before we eat?" I asked and Westley turned to me, winkles creasing his forehead. His eyes darted to the group of kids sitting around the fountain on the other side of the swing set then back to me. He shook his head, and I knew if the kids hadn't been there, he would have said yes. I could understand his hesitance, of course. Being a daddy and little, it was something special, something private. If the kids hadn't been here, maybe he would have wanted to play then. But having an audience complicated things. He couldn't act the way he wanted to. And it wouldn't be fun if he was uncomfortable.

But luckily for him, I had a way I could make it work. "They won't notice us, if that's what you're worried about," I told him and he pursed his lips.

"You mean to say that they wouldn't notice a big ass man like me playing on a kids' swing set?" His brows raised.

I bopped his nose in reprimand, saying, "Mind your language, my bunny. And yes, they won't notice."

He rolled his eyes and shook his head. I'd been right before; this boy would be a brat when he fully came into himself.

"Trust me, Westley. They won't notice a thing."

Wes sighed, as if he couldn't believe how stupid I was being. I gave him a firm look, and he immediately shook it off and gave me a smile. "Okay, but if they say anything . . ."

"They won't," I promised and Westley's chin lifted slightly before he got to his feet. I followed suit, taking his hand in mine once again. He squeezed my fingers as we walked over to the swing set, and I let some of my magic flow through me and into Westley. It was a simple bit of magic, something we used when we were working in the human world without wanting the humans to notice us. It didn't make us invisible, per se, just told the humans to look away from us. To not notice us.

We reached the swing set, and Westley glanced at the group of kids again. As I'd expected, they were looking anywhere but at us.

"See?" I asked and Westley shook his head.

"Just wait until I'm sitting on the swing, then they'll notice."

I pulled him to the closest swing and waved at him to get seated. He stared at it, as if expecting it to go down the moment he sat on it. Subtly, I checked the strength of the swing by pulling one of its chains. Being an elf gave me a bit more strength than the average human. And when the swing didn't break under my strength, I knew it was safe for my boy.

"Come on, I'll push you." I offered but Westley just rubbed the back of his neck.

"What? Don't do that. You'll end up pulling something," he argued but finally sat down, shooting another glance toward the kids who still hadn't looked at us.

I just shook my head before grabbing the base of the swing. "Ready?"

Westley glanced at me over his shoulder. "Will you stop if I say 'no'?"

I chuckled at the naughty boy. I pulled the swing toward me before letting it go. It was a slow swing, but with every push, Westley gained speed until he was grinning and whooping. He hadn't glanced at the kids once and that, more than anything, told me he was having fun. When we finally stopped, the sky had started to darken, night approaching as the sun set. Westley stood up and spun around. He threw his arms around me, and I could feel the joy and gratitude radiating from him, mirroring the way I felt about this beautiful boy. He hugged me tightly and I held him as long as I could. As long as he let me.

"Come on, let's eat. After you're done eating, I was thinking we could take a walk down to the docks before heading home."

"Sounds wonderful." A bright smile graced his face, his hazel eyes twinkling merrily.

Six

Westley

"This is perfect," I said around a bite of sandwich. Birch—could I call him Daddy now?—smiled as he watched me swallow before bringing a slice of apple to my lips.

"Open up," he said, a soft look in his eyes. I grinned as I bit my lip before opening my mouth for him. He slipped the juicy piece of apple between my lips, waiting for me to bite down. As soon as I'd bitten off half of the slice, he slipped the other half into his own mouth, making me smile. It was such a daddy thing to do, and it made me a bit more hopeful about where this would be going. It wasn't that I doubted him, but this was all new to me. I'd known I was a boy for a long time, but I'd never been able to find a daddy for myself. I knew I wasn't the typical little most daddies looked for, and to be honest, I'd given up on ever finding one for me. But looking at Birch, I felt hopeful again. I just prayed this hope wouldn't be in vain. I didn't think I could deal with it if Birch rejected me now.

We ate like that, with me eating my sandwich and Daddy slipping pieces of fruit into my mouth in between bites. As we ate, we talked. We talked about our favorite movies and books. About anything and everything that came to our minds. I told him about the bunnies at the shelter, and how I would adopt them if I could. I told him about my past experiences at the BDSM club in my old town, and we talked about what we liked in a daddy/boy relationship. We both leaned heavily toward the care-giving aspects of it, and I was surprised at how good of a match we made.

We had all kinds of first date conversations too, talking about things that I'd never talked about with anyone else before. It was nice. Just hanging out with Daddy and getting to know him. I was surprised by how much we had in common, like the theme songs Daddy liked. Disney movies and other cartoon movies too. Maybe it was because he was a daddy, and he was used to watching movies with his boy. The idea of Birch being with any other boy made my stomach sour, but it was his past. I couldn't begrudge him for having had boys before, could I? Sure, I didn't have much experience in that field, but that didn't mean I wanted him to have spent all these years alone too. He wasn't much older than me, but he had said that he'd known he was a daddy for a long time, so I didn't know how many boys he'd had, and I wasn't brave enough to ask.

Once we'd finished with our early dinner, Birch packed everything up as we decided to take that walk down to the docks.

"Come on, let's go." Birch stood up and offered me his hand and I smiled as I took it. He pulled me to my feet, and I stared at him in wonder. I wasn't the lightest guy and he'd pulled me up with no trouble at all. He didn't look all that big, and I was surprised he'd been able to do that. I wasn't going to comment on it, obviously. I didn't need to point out that I was much heavier than him. That fact was abundantly clear. He linked his fingers with mine, and I sighed happily as he led us out of the park.

I waited as he put the basket in the car's trunk before taking my hand into his once again. The sun had set already, but that didn't matter because I wasn't alone.

We set a steady pace, enjoying our surroundings as we went. I didn't know how much of Mistvale Birch had seen by now, but I hoped he liked what he saw. Mistvale was a lively town, and I loved living here. Finding a job at Rebba's place had been the luckiest thing that ever happened to me. I glanced over at Birch and corrected myself. It was the second luckiest thing that happened to me.

I wondered what it would be like to have him as my daddy all the time. To be able to go to him whenever I was feeling anxious. To always have him to hug me and hold me and tell me everything would be okay. I frowned as I realized there would still be some things that I wouldn't be able to experience. Birch was so much smaller than me. I couldn't exactly sit in his lap, could I? I didn't want to hurt him, but at the same time, I wished he could hold like that. Maybe if I lost some weight . . .

The musing led to all my insecurities roaring back to the forefront of my mind. Birch was amazing. He was handsome, rich, and had everything he could want. Why would he want someone like me? He could have anyone. What if, after a while, he decided he didn't need me anymore? That he didn't want me? What if he realized he could get so much better than me? What would I do then?

My heart hurt even imagining Birch with someone else, but would this really last?

"Daddy, are you sure?" The question popped out of my mouth before I could stop it, and I winced as we came to a stop.

Daddy turned me to face him, and I avoided looking into his eyes. I could feel him staring at me, and I let out a sigh as his finger touched my chin, tilting my face up so he could look at me.

"Sure about what, Westley?"

I bit my lip. I hadn't meant to ask him that, hadn't meant to remind him how much better he could do. I wanted to revel in what we had for as long as I could have it. But I guess I had gone and messed that up too.

"Are you sure that you want me? I know . . . I know I don't look like most boys do. I can understand if you don't want me for all the time, or if this is only . . . a fling or something." I shut my mouth because I knew if I didn't, I'd just keep talking and messing everything up even more. Birch was silent for a long moment, and my heart thundered in my chest as I waited for his reply.

I was still looking up at him, even though I wanted to do anything but, so I caught it when he raised his brow up at me. "Do I look like the other daddies, Little Bunny?"

I smiled at the nickname. I loved it when he called me that, and I hoped he would continue to use the name for much longer. It took me a moment to realize what he'd asked, and I shrugged my shoulders, shaking my head at the same time.

"So, do you not want me because I don't look like the other daddies?"

I shook my head vehemently. "Of course, I want you, Daddy. You're exactly the kind of daddy I want," I whispered. A warm smile spread across Daddy's face, softening his usually stern features.

"And you are exactly the kind of boy I want," he said, his voice a sweet, gentle caress against me. My eyes widened. Could someone—could *Birch*—really want a not-so-small little like me? I wasn't sure if questioning him would be the best course of action, and I really wanted to believe him. So, I smiled up at him, hoping he meant it. Hoping what we had wasn't something that would disappear in a few days.

"Okay, Daddy. I believe you," I said and he rubbed the top of my head with a small smile.

"Good boy."

My heart warmed in my chest at the pride in his voice. This. This was exactly what I wanted. Someone who was proud of me. Someone who would take care of me. Someone who *wanted* to take care of me. Not because he had to, but because he really wanted to. And it looked like I'd found him in Daddy. I just hoped I would never have to let him go.

Birch

By the time we arrived back at the pack land, it was clear Westley was tired. All I wanted to do was to take him home and tuck him into bed, cuddling him as he slept. But we weren't there yet, and I needed to be careful. Westley already doubted that I wanted him, really wanted him, and I needed to show him that I cared.

"You look tired, baby. How about I come inside and tuck you in before I leave? Would that be okay with you?" I asked as we reached the stoop of his cabin, and Westley looked up at me with a sleepy smile on his face.

"You will tuck me in? Really?" The excitement on his face made my heart hurt a little. How was it that something so simple made him so happy? I was now determined to spoil him as much as I could in the future because it was clear he deserved that and a lot more. Life hadn't been too kind to him, but I meant to change that.

He had told me a bit about his family over dinner, about how they'd kicked him out because he liked men. Things weren't like that with us elves. We were free to love whoever we wanted as long as the other person was consenting. But with the humans, it was different. There were people who couldn't deal with the fact that love had different forms. And I hated the fact that Westley's parents were some of them. My little bunny deserved the best in the world, and I hated that he'd had to deal with so much pain so early in his life. But I was here now, and I planned to take care of him for as long as he would let me.

"I'd love nothing more than to tuck you in, Little Bunny."

Westley leaned up on his toes and pressed his lips to mine, and I smiled at the sweet, fruity taste of him. I wrapped my arms around him and pulled him close as I slid my tongue into his mouth. He moaned, his voice a breathy whisper, and my arms tightened around him. I didn't want to let go. I never wanted to let go. But my boy was tired and he needed sleep. As his daddy, it was my job to put his needs before mine.

I pulled away with a soft sigh and smiled at the dazed look on Westley's face. "Come on, let's go in."

Westley nodded before opening the door to his cabin. I frowned when I realized it hadn't been locked. Westley needed to be careful. I knew the pack land was probably the safest place for him, that the other members of the pack would never let anyone sneak in. But still, leaving my boy unsafe like this didn't sit well with me.

"Why don't you lock your door?" I asked as we stepped inside. Westley closed the door behind himself, again, without locking it. He looked up at me with a smile and shrugged.

"There is only one entry into the farmland, and it is well guarded with security cameras and everything. I don't think anyone would sneak in here." Westley paused. "Why are you shaking your head? Anyway . . . even if they did, it's not like they'd find anything."

"But what about when you're inside? Do you lock the door then?" I asked and Westley scrunched his nose up adorably.

"Sometimes, I do. Don't worry, it's safe here. I wouldn't leave it open if I didn't believe it." I knew he meant it, and I let it go because he was right. There was no way anyone could sneak in here. If, someday in the future, we moved somewhere else, then I might insist on him locking the door, but for now, I let him be.

It was only once he was leading me into his bedroom that I realized I'd been making future plans for us already. One date, and I was already taken with him. But this connection I felt with him wasn't just my imagination. For the millionth time, I wished elves could sense their mates because I knew without a doubt that Westley was mine. If only I had a way to confirm it.

"Come on, let's get your teeth brushed and then get you changed into something comfy, okay?" When I didn't get a reply, I turned around to find him watching me with wide wet eyes. I rushed over to him and cupped his cheeks with my hands. "What's wrong? Why do you look so sad? What can I do?" I finally paused to take a breath as Westley snorted a laugh. I smiled at the wet sound and pressed my lips to his nose before pulling away. "Did I do something wrong, sweetheart? I need you to tell me."

Westley shook his head before his palms came up to rest over the back of my hands, pressing them more firmly to his cheeks. "You didn't do anything wrong, Daddy. I'm just overwhelmed, I guess. I've dreamed of this, of having a daddy, for so long, and now that you're here . . . It feels almost like I'm still dreaming. That I could wake up and all of this would disappear. And I'm scared of that. I don't want this to disappear, Daddy. I don't want you to disappear."

I pulled my little bunny into a hug and held him as he clung to me with all his might. I hated that my boy had been alone for so long, but I knew that his days of being alone had ended. Now that I was here, I planned on staying with him. My boy wouldn't go alone another day. I'd make sure of that.

"I'm not going anywhere, Little Bunny. I promise," I told him and led him into the bathroom so he could brush his teeth. It was a tad difficult with the wide smile that seemed like a fixture on his lips, but we managed. I left Westley to take care of his needs and went back into his bedroom. I walked over to the closet on the other side of his bed. One side of his closet was full of fuzzy, velvety clothes, and I realized my boy preferred soft clothes like that. Good to know.

When he got back from the bathroom, I dressed him in a pair of fuzzy pink shorts that looked adorable. I tilted my head as I tried to figure out if he needed a T-shirt, but he made the choice all on his own.

"Can I wear my cat onesie, Daddy?" he asked and I looked up at him as I caught the lilt in his voice. It had sounded softer, sweeter than the way he usually spoke. Did I finally get to meet his little?

"Of course, my sweet Little Bunny." I walked over to the closet and grabbed the onesie I'd spotted before.

Westley was watching me with wide, adoring eyes when I turned to walk back to him. Telling him to lean against me, I kneeled before him and helped him slip his feet into the legs of the onesie one by one. Once I was sure he wouldn't stumble, I stood up and helped him slip into the shirt and zipped it behind him.

When he was all dressed up, I pulled back and looked him over, smiling at how adorable he looked. "There. You look perfect and ready for bed. Come on, it's late. Let's get you tucked in," I said and Westley nodded before settling on the bed. I moved over to him and adjusted his pillow so he was comfortable. Like his couch, his mattress appeared old, and I hoped I would be able to get a home for the both of us soon. That reminded me, I needed to check out the housing options and figure out where we could stay once I moved here. But that was a worry for later.

I covered him with the blanket, tucking it into his sides until he was covered perfectly. I remembered something else I'd spotted in his cupboard and went back to get it. I grabbed the bunny I'd gotten him yesterday and carried it over to him. I tucked it into his side as well. Westley had said he regressed to five years old, so I didn't think he wanted a binky, but I would have to ask him later.

"Mr. Bunny will take care of you while I'm gone, okay Little Bunny?" I asked and Westley nodded softly, his eyes fluttering shut. It was clear he would be out in a minute, so I leaned over and pressed a soft kiss on his forehead before stepping back. "Good night, my sweet baby. I'll see you tomorrow." Westley mumbled a soft reply, but it was clear he was already half asleep. With a last smile at my boy, I left the room.

It was difficult to leave, but I made myself walk out the front door, closing it behind me. I wished I could lock it somehow, but I knew it wouldn't be necessary. Despite my fear that something might happen to my boy, the pack land was probably as safe as it could get. Telling myself to stop being so worried, I made my way over to my cabin. The night had gone better than I could have expected, and I couldn't wait to spend more time with Westley. I wanted to get to know him better, both his adult side and his little one. I wanted to know all about my boy and I couldn't wait. Even if I couldn't sense it, I was sure Westley was the one meant for me. He was perfect and there was no way he wasn't the one for me.

Seven

Westley

I dipped the paintbrush into the blue color before running it over the egg. Camille, Micah, and I were helping Birch get all the stuff ready for the party this Sunday. It was a fun activity, and if I'd been alone or if it had been just me and Birch, I would have probably slipped into my little persona. But since I was with Micah and Camille, I was just enjoying spending time with them painting some fake eggs. Apparently, these eggs would be hidden all over the farmland, and the kids who found the eggs would also find the card inside, telling them what gift they had won. It sounded like a fun game, and I was looking forward to watching it play out.

"So, I heard you found yourself a boyfriend, Westley," Camille said and I blushed as I shot Birch a glance before looking away. Camille had just finished telling us the story of how she had brought her dads together, and it seemed like she had a thing for matchmaking. Either that, or she just loved gossip. Were ten-year-olds supposed to be this nosy?

"I think so," I said as the old worry niggled in the back of my mind. Our date had gone well, better than I could've imagined. Birch had assured me that he really wanted me, and then he'd even tucked me into bed. I'd slipped into my little persona then, but Daddy hadn't commented on it, and I hadn't had a chance to be little again since.

Over the past few days, I'd gotten to know Birch even better. He was amazing, both as a person and as a daddy. But even as we grew closer, the worry started building in my head. What happened after the Easter party? Would he go back to wherever he had come from? Would he forget me? The questions filled my mind, making it so I couldn't enjoy the time we had together fully. Birch was special to me, more special than I'd ever expected him to be after such a short time together. I couldn't imagine losing him now, even though it had been barely a week since we started dating.

"What's wrong?" Micah asked, with that uncanny ability of his to sense whenever something was wrong. If I didn't know better, I would say he was reading my thoughts with the way he so accurately guessed stuff all the time.

"Nothing," I told them. I wasn't about to tell my worries to these two kids, now was I?

"I know what's wrong," Camille mused, a small smile tilting her lips. Her blue eyes were bright as they watched me, and I raised a brow at her in question, knowing there was no way she could know what I was thinking about.

"You like him a lot, don't you?" she asked, glancing up at Birch who was working on his laptop. We were in his cabin, since it was slightly bigger than mine and also had all the supplies for the party.

I watched him for a moment, his brows furrowed with concentration, a tiny little v forming between his brows that I just wanted to kiss. I was way over my head with him.

"Yeah, I like him a lot. But . . ." I stalled, unsure if this was something I wanted to talk about, especially with them. They were kids, not even teenagers yet. But I also knew that they were much older mentally than they looked. Defeating cancer and escaping a cult would do that to you, I supposed. I felt a strange kinship with these two, despite our age difference. Sometimes—who was I kidding?—most of the time, they were much easier to hang out with than adults. This was *not* one of those times.

"Go on," Micah urged, "we won't tell anyone. Your secret will be safe with us."

I sighed, rolling my eyes at their insistence. "It's nothing big. I'm just worried about what will happen after the party. Birch doesn't live here, and I don't know what he plans on doing once his work here is done."

Micah hummed softly and Camille smiled at me, that bright, cheerful smile that made me want to smile back.

"Well, I may be able to help with that," Micah said. "I overheard Papa and Noel talking about how Birch was planning on moving here. I don't think you need to worry about him leaving you."

Birch had said earlier that he was thinking of moving here. But I hadn't been sure. I'd also kind of forgotten about it. But now that Micah had said it, I clearly remembered Birch telling me that he had taken this project because he wanted to check out Mistvale, to figure out if it was the right place for him to move to. Did that mean we would stay together, even after the party was over? The thought made me immensely happy, and I hoped I wasn't the only one who was feeling this. I hoped Birch could feel just how special it was, how special we were. We still hadn't had the chance to play together, since Birch had been very busy with getting everything ready for the party. He had promised me that after the party was done, we would spend a whole day together as daddy and little. He'd said he had plans for me, and I couldn't wait to see what he had come up with.

But before that, we had a party to get everything ready for. And I needed to ask him once and for all to put my worries about the future to rest.

Birch

I glanced up at the three for the hundredth time, once again, ignoring the work I was supposed to be doing. Westley just looked so adorable sitting there with a paintbrush in his hand. I knew for a fact that if the other two kids hadn't been there, he would have slipped into his little role. I still hadn't had the pleasure of meeting Little Wes again after that night I'd tucked him in because I'd been so busy with preparations for the party. But I was determined to spend a whole day with him once the party was over.

I shook my head and forced myself to get back to work. I still needed to finalize the catering order and get all the decorations arranged. I wanted this party to be good for all the kids. It may not have been a big project originally, but now that my boy would be participating too, I needed to make sure it was the best party he had ever been to.

I also needed to look for a house in this town. There was no doubt in my mind now that I would be moving here, and I wanted to get a house as soon as possible so I could move Westley in with me. But before that, I had to tell him about the supes world, and I was worried how that would go. The only other humans I knew of who were aware of the supes were three of Noel's friends. He'd told me that one of his friends, a mage named Raphael, had a human mate, Jai. Jai and his brother were both aware of the supernatural world. William, one of Camille's dads had also been human when he found out about the supes. They'd all seemingly taken the revelation well, but I wasn't sure if it would be the same for Westley. What if he freaked out? What if he didn't want anything to do with me once he knew the truth? I had no clue how he would react, and I was scared shitless of telling him. But I knew I would have to because I could feel it. Westley was special. And even if he wasn't my mate, I still wanted him for as long as he would have me.

Once the kids had left, Westley hung around for a little bit before he was called away by Caleb. Now that they were finally gone, I could focus on my work. I ended up finishing it within a few minutes. Had I really been procrastinating for hours what I could've done in minutes? I shook my head, knowing it was all because of Westley. That boy had me wrapped around his finger, and I couldn't seem to bring myself to focus on anything when he was around.

"Hey, Birch. Got a minute?" Noel's voice called from the doorway and I looked up to find him standing there, glancing around at all the colorful stuff that was still littered around the room. The kids had ran as soon as I told them that it was time for cleanup, and Westley had helped until he had been called away, but now it was up to me to get rid of all the mess. I waved Noel inside as I turned off my laptop and stood up, stretching my stiff shoulders. I was used to desk work, and yet I never really enjoyed it. I guess it really was time to move on from that job, wasn't it? And now, I had the perfect reason for doing it too.

"What's up?" I asked Noel as I walked over to him.

"Oh, I just wanted to confirm that you're moving here, right?" Noel had a knowing glint in his eyes, and I raised a brow at him, even as I nodded.

"Yeah, I've decided to move here. Would you happen to know if there are any houses I can look into buying? Or where I might find information about them?"

"Well, if you want, you can live right here with us. We can build you two a new cabin and everything if you don't like one of the ones we have," Noel offered and I winced as I tried to figure out how to say no. Noel was such a sweet elf, it was hard to say no to him.

"That's very generous of you, Noel. But I'd prefer something closer to the town, and a bit more . . . private, I guess is the word. I hope you don't mind, but I just am not used to sharing my space like that."

"Oh, that's okay. Don't worry about it. I do think I saw a house near Cassian's place that had a 'for sale' sign. You know who Cassian is, right?"

I ran through all the people Noel had told me about before I remembered who he was. "The fire mage, right?" He was also Micah's father, if I remembered right.

"Yes, that's him. I saw a pretty cool townhouse near his place that I think you might like. I'll look into it and let you know, okay?"

I nodded in thanks. I still wasn't too familiar with Mistvale, and having Noel's help was nice.

"Do you need anything else, or would you like to help me with this?" I waved my hand around the mess that was my living room, and Noel shook his head, taking a step back.

"Oh no, I was just about to leave. I have a lot of work to do. But I also wanted to ask you to come over for dinner. I know you're worried about tomorrow's party, so I wanted to give you a chance to relax before the madness. I'll be cooking, and you can just hang out with all of us and relax, alright?"

"That sounds good. Thank you for all you've done to help me, Noel. I really appreciate it." Noel waved me off, shaking his head as if he had done nothing.

"Naw, I didn't do anything special. Plus, I'm really excited for this party too. It's gonna be amazing. You'll see. Now, dinner's at seven behind our cabin, okay? It will be a small affair. Just me, Caleb, you, Westley, Rebba and Devon." I was surprised since Noel seemed to have such a huge friend group, and all of them seemed to be completely involved in each other's lives. It was cute, actually. It was clear they cared about each other, and I liked that Westley lived in such a happy atmosphere.

"I'll be there," I assured him, and with a parting wave, he left the cabin. I looked around the living room, at all the paint bottles, the discarded eggs, and the finished ones that were placed in a big basket. It would definitely take me a few hours to clean up all of this. But still, I was smiling as I cleaned because I couldn't wait to see Westley again. Yeah, I was definitely wrapped around his finger and I didn't mind it one bit.

Eight

Westley

The party was in full swing, and I was having the time of my life. After spending the last few days helping Daddy get everything together for the party, I was proud of how well we'd put everything together. Helping him with the arrangements had also given me the opportunity to get to know him better, and I was feeling more and more sure that Birch could be my forever daddy. He was everything I'd ever wanted, ever needed, and he seemed to want me just as much. What more could I ask for?

I'd been hesitant about participating at first. After all, I was an adult and this party was for kids. But then, Micah and Camille had dragged me off with them, and soon enough, I'd been as involved in the party as them. I'd already found an Easter egg, one of the ones Micah had painted. And according to the card inside it, I would soon be getting a new plushie. I was so excited. You could never have enough plushies.

Now, we were getting ready for a game of Eggs and Spoons. Basically, we had to carry an egg on a spoon by holding the spoon in our mouth and carrying it over to the finish line. Obviously, the goal of the game was to not drop the egg while doing it. I felt like I might be able to win this one. We'd already played the sack run, where I'd jumped like a frog to get to the finish line. Camille had beaten me in that one. But this game, I was determined to win. The prize for winning any of the games was a huge basket full of goodies made by the Easter company Daddy was the CEO of.

Just before the race started, I looked up and my eyes met Birch's. Over the course of the day, I'd found him looking at me almost every time I looked up. He had a soft little smile on his face, and knowing it was for me made my day a hundred times better.

Having Daddy watch me as I played made the games even more fun. I stuck the spoon into my mouth and took a deep breath before balancing the egg on top of it. Gus was refereeing this game, so to speak, and he stood near the finish line with a wide grin on his face. Once everyone was ready, a whistle blew from somewhere—courtesy of Caleb, if I had to guess—and everyone started racing toward the finish line. I tried to run as steadily as possible so I wouldn't drop the egg while still maintaining enough speed that I might stand a chance to win.

I heard a splat to my right and realized Cam was already out of the game. I'd expected as much, since she was so impatient. I tried not to grin—and end up dropping my egg—as I hustled forward. The embarrassment I'd felt while participating in the first game was long gone. The kids didn't find it weird that an adult was playing with them. Instead, it made them even more excited. The adults didn't seem to mind that I was playing with their kids, either. Other than Micah and Camille, I didn't know any of the other kids. But Noel had told me that they were all kids from the town, and it was fun having the place so crowded for once. Don't get me wrong, crowds weren't really my thing usually, but kids I could handle.

I didn't even realize I'd crossed the finish line until Gus jumped up shouting, "Westley is the winner!" This time, I did grin as I pulled the spoon and egg away from my mouth. Before I could open my mouth to say anything, arms wrapped around me and the familiar scent of expensive cologne surrounded me.

"You won, my Little Bunny. Congratulations." I grinned as I wrapped my arms around him and returned the hug. It was stupid to be this happy about winning a game against a bunch of kids. But I couldn't stop myself from laughing in delight as Birch held me. It was easy to lose myself in the moment, and frankly, in all the fun. As long as the others didn't mind, I would celebrate my win.

"I did win, Daddy. Will I get a reward later?" I whispered in his ear, and his arms tightened around me before he pulled away. I looked up to find him grinning at me, and I gave him my best puppy eyes, to which he just laughed.

"I'll think about it. Now go play some more games. When you're tired, just come over to me, okay?"

I nodded before racing off to where Micah and Camille were waving me toward them.

The party went on for hours, and I couldn't remember the last time I'd had so much fun. Around four in the afternoon, all the kids except Micah and Camille had finally left, and I was tired down to my little toes. Now, all I wanted to do was go home and cuddle with my daddy, but it didn't look like he'd be free for another few hours.

Daddy walked over to me as I sat in one of the chairs gathered around the clearing. I'd just meant to spend a few minutes resting before I helped everyone with the cleanup, but I didn't feel like I could get up. I hadn't realized how much energy I had expended, but now I really wanted to sleep.

"Hey, Little Bunny. Are you tired?" Daddy asked and I looked up to find him standing before me. When had he come here? How had I not noticed him? Was I really that tired?

"Yeah, Daddy. But I'll help with the cleanup in a minute. I promise," I assured him and he shook his head, a smile on his face.

"There are more than enough people here to help with the cleanup, Westley. Why don't you go back to the cabin and change into some comfortable clothes. I'll be there as soon as I'm done here and help you get ready for bed. I'll bring you some dinner too."

I frowned. I really wanted to do what he was telling me to do. But I also didn't want to leave them to do all the work after I'd spent the day having fun. "I don't mind helping, Daddy. I can go after a little while."

Daddy sank to his knees in front of me and took my hands in his smaller ones. "Who's the daddy here?" he asked and I sighed.

"You, of course."

"And who's the boy?"

My brows furrowed as I reminded him, "Me. I'm the boy."

"And what do good boys do?" he asked and I shook my head at all these questions. I was so tired. I didn't want to answer these questions. But I knew the answer. Of course, I did.

"Good Boys listen to their Daddies," I answered and Daddy smiled widely at me.

"That's right. So, go back home and get changed into comfy clothes. Cuddle on the couch or in your bed with your bunny, and I'll be there with dinner in a bit. Okay?"

I sighed, knowing Daddy wouldn't budge. So, despite wanting to help, I shuffled to my feet and made my way to my cabin. Even though I wanted to help, I couldn't stop smiling as I entered my cabin. The way Daddy had taken care of me was everything I'd been looking for, and I couldn't wait for tomorrow, when Daddy and I would play together for the first time.

Birch

The party had gone way better than I'd expected. For one, I hadn't expected as many kids as the number that had shown up. For a town this small, there had been a lot of them. I'd also realized that I may have not been the perfect candidate for this job. Thank God it was the only time I planned on doing it. I wasn't the best with kids. Even though I adored littles, actual children were a completely different species. Even so, the party had gone off without a hitch, and I knew I'd be recommending the others at The Easter keep doing parties like this one every year. It was a new opportunity to spread some joy, and that was the whole point of our company.

I also hadn't been able to keep my eyes away from my boy. Westley had seemed to flourish as he played all the games along with the other children. I was thankful to Micah and Camille for making Westley feel comfortable enough and encouraging him to play with them. I'd loved watching the joy on Westley's face as he played all the games, and he had been so excited when he'd won. I smiled as I remembered his request for a reward, and I knew I'd be giving him the best reward possible.

I looked around the clearing, thankful for Noel and his friends as they hurried around cleaning everything up. Gus, Micah's father, was a blur as he rushed around gathering up all the garbage. It was a strange sight, watching a vampire clean up kids' messes, but I'd soon realized that Gus wasn't the typical vampire. The guy was smiling all the time. I mean, I'd expected him to be smiling since this was a party, but still. Every time I looked at him, he was either smiling or laughing. His mate Cassian, on the other hand, seemed to smile only when Gus was around. Or Micah. If the house Noel had been talking about was the one for me, these two would be my new neighbors.

"That was a great party." I turned to look at the man who had spoken and realized it was Camille's father. It took me a moment to realize what he was, and when I did, I had to concentrate on not showing him my surprise. He was a dragon. I'd never expected to meet a dragon in my life. As far as I knew, they'd stopped socializing hundreds of years ago, preferring to live deep in the forests in their dragon forms. And yet here he was, living life as a human.

"Thank you. I couldn't have done it alone. Raiden, right?" The man smiled at me, his gray eyes twinkling as he nodded. His eyes were the color of the sky, and I wondered what kind of dragon he was. If I had to guess, I would say a storm or a wind dragon. "Camille was a big help," I said and his smile widened a little.

"She hasn't stopped talking about the party since we first learned of it, so I'm sure she did all she could to help."

I nodded at him as I tried to figure out where I could find some dinner for my boy. Noel had said he made food earlier so we could eat once the party ended, but I wasn't sure where he had put everything.

"Oh, I almost forgot. Congratulations on finding your mate." My eyes jerked to Raiden as I realized what he had said. It was true, then? Westley was my mate.

A wide smile spread across my face, and I almost hugged the man before remembering that he was practically a stranger and wouldn't appreciate it. "Thank you so much. You can sense it, then? The bond?" I asked, wondering how he had known.

"There's not a lot that is hidden from me, Birch. I've lived a long life and gained many experiences. I sensed the bond when I saw the two of you together earlier."

My heart was thundering wildly in my chest as the knowledge sank in. Westley was my mate. My little bunny would stay with me forever. What more could I have asked for?

Now, I just needed to figure out how to tell him about the supes. About the world he lived in without knowing anything about it. It would be tough, and I had no idea how Westley would react. But I did know that I would be right there waiting until he came to terms with it. Now that I knew for certain he was my mate, there was no way I would ever let him go.

Nine

Westley

Daddy would be here any minute, and I couldn't wait to get started. It had been so long since I sank into my little space, since I had a playdate, and I was super excited for today. It was going to be my first playdate with Daddy, and I was hopeful it would go better than the past few dates I had been on. It had been a while since I'd been on a playdate, mostly because I'd gotten tired of the same thing. Most daddies didn't want a little like me, and they almost never hesitated to tell me that. Of course, the way they told me was kind enough. After all, they were still daddies, even if none of them wanted to be my daddy. But still, I knew I wasn't most people's preferred little. But, if Daddy Birch was to be believed, I was exactly his type. And I hoped he meant that because I couldn't change. I had tried and it had just made me sad. I liked eating and I wasn't unhealthy, just a bit bigger than most. That couldn't be so bad, could it?

I shook my head, reminding myself that Daddy Birch liked me just like I was. He'd said so himself, and if I couldn't believe myself, I had to believe him because Daddy was always right.

The knock on my door had me grinning and jumping on my toes as I raced toward the front door. My little side was so close to the surface I knew I would be jumping headlong into our date the moment I saw him. I jerked the door open and melted as Daddy smiled at me in that adoring way of his. He was dressed in faded jeans and a soft-looking blue T-shirt, his hair slicked back as always. I wondered if he would let me rub my cheek along his beard.

"Daddy, you're here!" I squealed as I jumped into his arms, practically throwing myself at him, and he laughed, a loud happy sound as he wrapped his arms around me. I vibrated in his arms, eager to start our day, and he never once let go or told me I was too heavy to be hanging off him. I pulled away when I decided our hug had been long enough and grabbed his hand, pulling him into the house with me.

"Oh Daddy! I'm so excited for today. What are we going to do? Can I play with my toys? I love trains! And animals! And my stuffies. Oh, and I love coloring too."

I jumped around the room before rushing back to him and grabbing both of his hands. He was just standing there, smiling widely at me, and I wanted to shake him so he would say something. "Daddy! What are we gonna do?"

"First things first, my Little Bunny. I need to give my bunny a kiss." Daddy pulled me close to him and pressed a big smooch on my forehead, making me giggle. I pulled away from him and looked up into his eyes and at the wide smile on his face. Daddy looked so happy. Was that really because of me?

"Alright, Little Bunny. We need to get you dressed for play-time. Let's go find something for you to wear." Daddy pulled me along with him as he walked into my bedroom. I dropped his hand and hopped on the bed and got settled. I swung my legs as I waited for him to find me clothes.

"Can I wear my onesie, Daddy? The bunny one?" I asked. The bunny onesie was my absolute favorite and I loved wearing it. It made me feel all soft and warm.

Daddy shuffled through my clothes before pulling out a different onesie. This one had a panda hood and I liked it too. Not as much as the bunny one, but close.

"How about this one? The bunny one is still in the laundry basket from the other day."

"Oops. I don't want to wear dirty clothes. So I guess this one is okay."

Daddy smiled before closing the closet and walking over to me. He placed the onesie beside me on the bed before tapping my shoulder.

"Arms up," he said and I pulled my arms up so Daddy could remove my T-shirt. Daddy dressed me quickly and efficiently, even though I kept wriggling because I just wanted to play. I couldn't wait to show Daddy all my toys, and I wanted him to play with me too.

"You will play with me Daddy, right?" I asked. I'd never played with a daddy before and I wanted to play with Daddy Birch. I always wanted to play with Daddy Birch.

"I'd be honored to play with you, Little Bunny. There. You look absolutely adorable. Should I call you little panda now?"

I scrunched up my nose. I loved being Daddy's Little Bunny. I didn't want to be a panda. I shook my head, and Daddy smiled at me before ruffling my short hair.

"I guess I have my answer, then. You're my Little Bunny, for now and forever. Alright?" I really hoped Daddy meant that because I planned on never, ever letting him go.

"I promise."

Back in the living room, Daddy glanced at the blanket where I'd spread out all the toys I had and turned back to me with a smile. "Let's see what toys you have."

I nodded and tightened my hand around his and pulled him over to the blanket. I showed him my train set, and my stuffies.

"Look at the plushie, Daddy. It's so smooth. I got it at the party yesterday. And look at this!" I showed Daddy the basket I'd won at the party and all the little toys I found inside.

For the next few hours, I completely lost myself in my toys. I played with Daddy and I couldn't remember the last time I had so much fun. Playing with Daddy was so easy, and I didn't have to worry about anything as we carried animals from one train station to the other with my train set. We made up stories for them and rescued them from evil princesses.

Daddy excused himself after a while, telling me he needed to make lunch and insisting I keep playing when I offered to help. I wasn't used to staying little for so long without worrying about anything, but with Daddy, it was all so easy. When Daddy finally called me over for lunch, I washed my hands quickly and shuffled over to the small dining table. I smiled at the food Daddy placed in front of me. There were chicken nuggets, a big portion of mac 'n' cheese, and some peas that I really didn't want to eat. I didn't have any special plates, but Daddy had still set the food in portions like you would in special plates. I also had a mug of milk with the food.

"I'll get you a special plate next time, okay Little Bunny?" I nodded happily and stuffed my face with food as I told him what we would do after I was done eating. I had a lot of plans for today.

I wanted to play more, but I'd started feeling sleepy by the time I finished lunch, and Daddy decided it was time for a nap.

After putting the dishes in the sink, Daddy guided me over to the bedroom, his hand a warm support on my lower back.

Daddy helped me lay down on the bed before covering me with the blanket. I was sleepy and yet, I couldn't bring myself to sleep, because I didn't want to waste even a second of this date. "Will you tell me a story, Daddy?"

Birch

"I'd love to tell you a story, my Little Bunny." I slid into the bed beside him, sitting up with my back to the headrest so Westley could cuddle into my side. He placed his head on my thigh, and I smiled as I ran my fingers through his short hair.

I realized this was as good an opportunity as I would get to tell Westley a little bit about myself. "So, this story is going to be about an elf and Little Bunny."

"I'm Little Bunny!" he gasped in delight, his eyes wide in realization. I couldn't help but chuckle at the surprised look on his face, and I pulled him into my side, my arm wrapping tightly around his back.

"That's right. So, shall I continue? Or will you keep interrupting?" I winked at him to show him I was teasing, and he grinned up at me.

"Please continue, Daddy. I promise I won't interrupt again."

"Good boy. Now, the story starts when the elf moves to a new city looking for his forever love. See, in the elf's world, every person gets their perfect match. They're called their mates. Every magical person has a Fated mate, and the elf spent years looking for his without ever finding him. He had almost given up hope because he didn't think he would ever find him, but then, he does."

"Was Little Bunny his mate?" Westley asked, his voice full of awe and childish excitement.

I smiled at him, my heart feeling so warm and full. I knew I couldn't tell him yet since it would be too fast by human standards, but I loved Westley already. I loved him with my whole heart, and I was so grateful to Fate for giving him to me. "You're right. Little Bunny was his mate. Except, there was a small problem."

"Oh no! What was the problem, Daddy?"

"Well, you see, humans didn't know about magical creatures, didn't know things like forever mates existed. So, how was the elf to tell his mate that they belonged together?" Westley hummed thoughtfully, and I waited for him to speak because it was clear he was thinking something.

"I think, if the elf told Little Bunny the truth, he would believe him. I mean, Little Bunny likes the elf too, right?"

"That's right, sweetheart. They both love each other. So, should I continue the story?" Westley grinned sheepishly at me, and I smiled at him as I continued. "So, after the elf fell in love with Little Bunny, he asked his friend to help him prove to his bunny that magic existed. See, the elf's friend was a shifter. He could turn into an animal. So, with the help of his friend, the elf was able to prove that magic was real to his bunny. And when Little Bunny finally believed him, the elf was able to claim him and make Little Bunny his forever. And then they lived happily ever after."

"I loved that story, Daddy! Thank you for telling it to me. Will you tell it to me again sometime?" Westley yawned widely, and I smiled as I pulled him even closer to me. His breathing deepened almost instantly, and within minutes, he was out like a light. He had taken it well, but then again, I'd told it like it was a story. What would he say when I told him that the story had been real? Would he be as ready to believe as he'd been now? Or would the rational part of him tell him I was lying?

After a few minutes of watching Westley sleep, I shifted out of the bed carefully so I wouldn't wake him and made my way to the kitchen. I quickly washed up the dishes before heading to the couch in the living room. I would let Westley sleep for another hour and read in the meantime.

I grabbed my tablet from the table where I'd left it when I first arrived and opened the book I'd been reading. I was pretty sure I would be telling Westley the truth tonight, if only because I didn't want to keep it hidden anymore. Now that I knew for a fact Westley was my mate, I didn't want any secrets between us.

I opened my text messages and shot Noel a text, asking him if I could borrow his mate to show Westley that magic existed. I figured nothing would be more demonstrative than having a shifter shift right in front of him. Once that was done, I turned back to my ebook and tried to focus on it. Whatever Westley's reaction was, I knew I would accept it, because as his Daddy, my number one duty was to do what was best for him.

I heard shuffling in the bedroom some forty minutes later, and I was just about to go check on Westley when he walked out of the bedroom, dressed in a pair of sweatpants and a soft T-shirt. It looked like he was back to being an adult, and I was thankful for it even though I'd loved spending time with little Westley today. I needed to tell him the truth, and I hadn't wanted to risk ripping him out of his little space.

"Hey Westley, how was your nap? Sleep okay?" I asked, putting my e-reader away and turning to him as he took a seat beside me. I pushed down the nerves that threatened to overcome me as he gave me a hesitant smile, his hands clasped tightly on his lap.

"That was the best nap of my life, Daddy. Thank you for staying with me."

I wanted to tell him I'd stay with him forever, but I wouldn't until I had told him the truth so he would know that I really meant it. Which brought me to my current dilemma. I needed to tell him the truth, but I didn't want him to freak out on me. I didn't know what I would do if he was afraid of me.

"Westley, there is something I need to tell you."

Westley froze in his seat, and his eyes widened slightly as he looked at me before glancing away almost instantly.

His eyes focused on the couch as he spoke, a tremor in his voice. "Did I do something wrong? I promise I didn't mean to. If you tell me what I did wrong, I promise I'll get better at it. Did you not like my little side? It's okay. We can be only adults if y—"

"Westley. Stop."

Westley snapped his mouth shut and I shook my head, wishing he wasn't so hard on himself. I guess it would be my job as his daddy to make sure his insecurities never came between us.

"Westley, let me start by saying that today was amazing. It was better than I could've imagined, and it was all because of you. I love spending time with you, both as a little and like this. That's not what this is about. I just need to tell you something, and I hope you won't freak out."

I could see that Westley wanted to say something, but he kept his mouth shut like I told him to, and I smiled at him, proud of him for listening to me.

"You're such a good boy for listening to Daddy and staying quiet. Do you remember the story I told you before you fell asleep?"

Westley's brows furrowed as he tried to remember and then he nodded. "I remember."

"Well, that story is true."

"Well, I thought it was. I mean it was based on you and me, right?"

"It was. But what I mean is . . . the elf and the shifter parts. Those were true too." I waited for him to realize it, to realize what I was saying, and when he did, his eyes widened and he shook his head, as if he couldn't bring himself to believe it. I couldn't blame him for not believing me. It was pretty unbelievable, especially for a human.

Ten

Westley

What was Daddy saying? Elves were real? Was Daddy saying he was like one of those Christmas elves who run around packing gifts for everyone?

That couldn't be true. Daddy must be thinking I was still little, and that was why he was saying all these crazy things. Elves? Shifters? Magic? Those things only existed in books, in stories. They couldn't be here in real life.

"I'm not little right now, Birch. You realize that, right?" I asked softly. It felt weird calling him by his name after I'd been calling him Daddy all day, but I wanted him to know how very not-little I was right now. The weirdest thing was, Daddy didn't look like he was joking. It didn't look like he was telling a story. The way he was watching me, as if waiting for me to freak out, told me he didn't mean it as joke. Did he really believe he was an elf? I liked Daddy Birch, but had I been too hasty? Had I ended up with a crazy guy for a daddy?

There was a knock on the door before I could respond, so I got up to open it. A wave of cigarette smoke blew in, and I found Devon standing on the other side.

"Hey Devon, did you need anything?" From all the people who lived around the farmland, I was probably the closest to Devon after Noel. Devon was a quiet man and never talked much. But that was exactly what made us such good friends because I could talk for hours without needing anyone else to speak a word.

"I'm actually here to help Birch. Noel thought it would be easier if it was me instead of Caleb. Bobcats aren't as scary, you know?"

I didn't know. "Um, I'm super confused right now. What's going on?"

Devon stepped past me into the cabin, and I closed the door before turning to him. His long black hair was braided down his back, the purple and turquoise streaks glinting in the low light of my cabin. The man was gorgeous, but even after spending months with him, I barely knew anything about him. He never talked much about himself, even though he made a point of making sure everyone on the farmland was happy and didn't need anything.

"Remember the shifter from my story, Westley?" Daddy asked and I sighed. He was still stuck on that story. But I couldn't lie to Daddy or ignore him so I nodded, and he waved at Devon. "Devon here is a bobcat shifter. He's going to shift in front of you so you know magic is real."

This couldn't be happening. What was going on? Had I somehow fallen into a fairytale? One where Daddy was the prince charming, and I was the prince in distress? I shook my head, still not wanting to believe this. How could I believe him? It just seemed so . . . well, crazy! Elves and shifters?

Next, Daddy would say there were vampires in this world!

My eyes widened as Devon started unbuttoning his shirt, and I glanced at Daddy. "What's he doing?"

"Dude, I don't want to waste another outfit. If I shift now, I'll end up ripping all my clothes," Devon said in his usual soft voice. I shook my head at another bit of crazy and waited. I had no clue what I was waiting for. How the hell would Devon shift? Was it going to be like some kind of magic trick they did at children's birthday parties?

Once Devon was down to his underwear, his back to us, he spoke, "Now, look carefully. Don't tell me later that it was some kind of trick of the light. This is real, Westley. And I'm glad I finally get to tell you. I don't like keeping secrets."

I took a deep breath. Even though I didn't believe all of this, I could feel the seriousness of the moment in the air, and I watched carefully as Devon took a deep breath.

It barely took a minute, maybe half of one. Where Devon stood just a minute ago, now there was a sandy bobcat, watching me with the same pale-blue eyes that Devon had. His ears flicked and his nose twitched as he waited for me to react.

Well, crap. It looked like Daddy hadn't been lying.

Magic was real.

One of my best friends was a bobcat.

My daddy was an elf.

Crap. I was going to faint.

Birch

Shit. Today may have been a bit too much for my little bunny. I shouldn't have told him everything. Maybe I should have waited until we knew each other better before telling Westley the truth. But what was done was done, and now I needed to take care of my boy.

I turned to the bobcat. "Thank you for your help, Devon. I really appreciate it."

Devon walked over to the couch where I'd placed an unconscious Westley and licked his cheek before walking over to the door. It was clear what he wanted, and I hurried over to the door to open it for him. He left after one last glance at Westley, and I grabbed his clothes and folded them before placing them out on the porch for him.

Once that was taken care of, I picked Westley up and carried him into the bedroom. Just as I was placing him on the bed, his hand wrapped around mine and he looked up at me.

"That's why." His voice was a weak whisper, and I pulled my hand away so I could press my palm to his forehead. He wasn't too warm, which I was thankful for. He wouldn't be able to get sick once he was mated to me, but for now he was human, and humans were extremely susceptible to a lot of dangerous illnesses.

"What? What's why?" I asked as I took a seat beside him, hesitating to touch him because I wasn't sure if he would still be okay with it. He answered the question for me by grabbing my hand and pulling it closer to him. He clutched my palm between both of his and smiled up at me.

"That's why you are able to carry me everywhere, why you can let me sit on your lap without getting tired. Because you have magic. You're stronger than you look because of it, aren't you?"

I smiled at the question, realizing I hadn't given him as much credit I should have. Even though it had been a shock for him, he didn't seem to fear me. And that was all I'd wanted. "Yeah,

I'm stronger and faster than I look. An elf's magic is subtle, not as clear in what it can do as a shifter's or a vampire's."

Westley's eyes widened as I spoke and he shook his head. "So, vampires are real, then?"

I chuckled and nodded. "Actually, one of your friends is a vampire." I wondered if he could guess who.

"Oh wow, really? Let me guess. Is Cassian one of them?" I shook my head and he got a thoughtful look on his face again. "William, then? Camille's dad?" I shook my head again and he growled. "Tell me!"

"Cassian is actually a fire mage. And William is . . . well, he's something. I can't get a read on him, so you'll have to ask him or Cam. But Cassian's mate, on the other hand, is a vampire." Westley sputtered for a second, as if what I'd said was even more unbelievable than the fact that magic existed in the first place.

"That can't be true! Gus is a vampire? I thought vampires were all grumbly and angry like Cassian! Gus is so . . . so happy all the time! How can he be a vampire?"

I laughed at the disgruntled look on his face before shaking my head. "Of course, he's happy, sweetheart. He has his Fated mate with him, and they even have a son. Of course, he's happy."

Westley's eyes widened as they met mine and he sat up. "Oh, I remember you saying something about Fated mates in the story. Was that true too? That there is a perfect match for everyone? And that . . . that I'm yours?"

I nodded, my heart thundering in my chest as I waited for him to either accept or reject our bond. Since we hadn't claimed each other yet, it would be possible to break the bond if he didn't want it. Not that I wanted to break our bond, but

I would if that was what he wanted, if he couldn't deal with all these new things.

"But, I'm human. How does that work?"

"If you accept our bond, we will claim each other. And once we do, some of my magic will be transferred to you. You will be able to stay healthy always and have my immortality, too."

"Immortality? So, I will live forever?" Westley gasped and I nodded. "Wow, that's amazing. And . . . you will stay with me for always? You won't get bored?"

"Never," I promised. "Westley, Fate picked you for me because you're my perfect match, my other half. There is no way, no reason, I would ever want to leave you. You were made for me, just like I was made for you. Okay?"

"Okay. You have to give me a bit of time to actually accept this, you know? I spent so long thinking I would never find the one, that I would always be alone because of what I look like and the fact that I am a little. But now you are telling me that you were made just for me, and I want to believe it but it's difficult."

"I'll give you all the time you need, Westley. Because we have forever together, and I'm going to spend all of it with you."

Westley smiled at me before resting his head on my shoulder, and then he proceeded to ask me a million questions about magic, about the supernatural, about this town. I was only too happy to answer as many of them as I could.

Late in the night, after what felt like hours of talking, he asked his final question.

Westley looked up at me, his hazel eyes shining in the moonlight since we'd forgotten to turn on the lights. His palm came up to rest on my cheek, his fingers scratching through my beard. His voice was a whisper as he asked, "Will you claim me, Daddy? Will you make sure you're mine forever?"

And how could I ignore a sweet request like that?

Eleven

Westley

"Are you sure you don't want to wait and get to know each other better first?" Daddy asked softly, his dark eyes full of adoration as they roamed over me. My first thought was that he wasn't as attracted to me as I was to him, and that was why he wanted to take it slow. But then I reminded myself that he was my Daddy, and daddies were always thinking about what was best for their boys.

"I want you, Daddy. I want to be yours forever. Please claim me," I whispered and Daddy watched me for another moment before a wide, beautiful smile spread across his lips.

He slid under the covers beside me, both of us still fully clothed. He lay on his side and I turned to face him, my eyes meeting the dark pools that made me want to drown in them and never surface.

"Oh, Westley. You're all my dreams come true. I can't wait to spend forever with you. I love you, Little Bunny."

I gasped at his declaration. The rational part of my mind tried to tell me that it was too soon, but it had already been proven wrong once when Devon turned into a bobcat so I ignored it. Daddy Birch was everything I'd ever wanted, and his love for me was clear in his eyes, in each soft caress of his palm down my side.

"I love you, too, Daddy. I never knew I could be this happy, that I could have everything I'd ever wanted. I want to be your boy forever."

Daddy's arm wrapped around my waist as he pulled me closer, and I sank into him. I breathed in the scent of his cologne as he pressed his lips to mine and then I was just gone. Drowning in the warmth, the pleasure, the intensity of his kiss. The way his lips caressed mine, his tongue catching me by surprise as I moaned my pleasure.

Daddy pushed me on my back and climbed over me, his palm running over every inch of me he could reach. My fingers curled into his hair, and I held on tight so he wouldn't pull away, my other hand playing with the coarse hair of his beard.

Carefully, he untangled my fingers from his hair and pulled away, sitting up with his knees on either side of me and I whined. I wanted him back.

Daddy shushed me, grabbing the hem of my T-shirt and raising a brow at me. As if he even had to ask. I nodded instantly, and he grinned as he pulled the shirt over my head, his eyes roaming over all my uncovered skin.

I had the sudden urge to cover myself up. My chest was hairless, and I was chubby all over, with a bit of extra padding around my waist. What if Daddy didn't like what he saw?

The question had barely crossed my mind when Daddy groaned, this low sound that seemed to emanate from deep in his throat. He ran his fingers from the arch of my neck all the way down to the waistband of my pants, scorching my skin wherever he touched. With just a single touch, Daddy made me feel treasured and safe and like I was his.

I glanced up from where I'd been following the progress of his fingers, and his dark gaze bore into me, holding me captive as he pulled his shirt off and threw it behind him.

My eyes dropped to his chest instantly, and I swallowed as I took him in. He was . . . built. I'd felt him, of course. All that muscular hardness, but it was a hundred times better without the cloth barrier.

I raised my arm up toward him, wanting him to touch me, wanting to touch all that glorious skin he'd revealed. I wanted to run my fingers through the coarse brown hair on his chest. I wanted to feel his chest hair rubbing against my chest.

Daddy covered me with his body, and I moaned when his warm skin met mine. Our erections were perfectly lined up as Daddy claimed my lips and rocked into me, his hips setting a maddeningly slow rhythm that matched his kisses.

My palms traced the straining muscles of his shoulders and his back, rubbing up and down as he rocked into me. His taste was heavy on my tongue and I needed more. I needed all of him. I needed him to take me, to mark me, to make me his.

My fingers sank under the waistband of his jeans and dug into his ass, forcing him to increase his pace. I moaned when his dick rubbed against mine just right, causing sparks shoot down my spine.

In the next moment, Birch pulled away, and I was left feeling cold and empty. My eyes fluttered open—I hadn't even realized I'd closed them—and I looked up to find him staring at me with a raised brow.

"Why did you stop?" I whined and he narrowed his eyes at me.

"I stopped because you need to remember who the daddy is." He pointed at himself. "I'm Daddy. Which means I set the pace. I will claim you tonight, Westley, but do not rush me, okay?"

I nodded mutely, goosebumps racing down my arms as he stared at me in that intense way of his.

"Good. Now let's get you out of these pants, and then I'll tell you exactly what I plan on doing to you."

I shivered as Daddy's fingers slid beneath my waistband. Staring me right in the eye, he proceeded to pull my pants and underwear down my legs. He removed my pants and threw them behind him, just like he'd dumped his T-shirt before.

His fingers ran down my thighs, raising goosebumps as they went. His long fingers were firm against my skin, digging in just a little to make sure I knew exactly where he was touching me. It was more erotic than I'd expected it to be, and my dick leaked steadily on my stomach as he kept skimming his fingers up and down my legs.

"I'm going to taste you now, my sweet bunny." That was all the warning I got before Daddy slid down the bed and pulled my dick into his mouth in one smooth move. I gasped as the wet heat of his mouth enveloped my dick, wondering if I'd died and gone to heaven because goddamn that felt so good. My hips jerked upward of their own accord, but Daddy's tight grip on them kept me from pushing deeper into his mouth.

Just like before, Daddy set a slow, maddening pace as he sucked my dick, his tongue licking up my slit and wrapping around my head. He moaned deep in his throat, and it took all of my control to not shoot right then. But I didn't want to come unless Daddy had told me to, so I tried to keep my orgasm at bay. I didn't think it could get any better than this, but then Daddy proved me wrong by swallowing me all the way in. The tip of my dick pressed against the back of his throat, and my fingers curled into the bedsheet beneath me as I tried desperately not to push even deeper into his mouth. A part of me still found it unbelievable that Daddy was giving me a blowjob. But it was very real. The way his mouth surrounded me, enveloping me in a blazing warmth, was marvelous.

"Daddy, please stop. You're going to make me cum." I groaned and Daddy pulled away from my dick to give me a wicked smile.

"You're such good boy for letting Daddy know. As a reward, I will allow you to come whenever you want to, boy. Just this once. After all, I have all night to play with you." I moaned loudly at his words, so loud I would have been embarrassed if I hadn't been hanging on by my fingertips.

Before I could even think about forming a reply, Daddy pulled me into his mouth once more, and this time I couldn't stop myself from pushing up into him. Despite his grip on my hips, I managed to set a slow pace as I pushed into his mouth repeatedly. I knew it was only because he allowed it that I was able to, but I kept pushing into his mouth until I could feel that tingle down my spine, telling me I would cum at any moment. Daddy pulled away from my dick, and as I was just about to complain, his hand replaced his mouth. He jacked me furiously as he crawled up my body and kissed me with just as much intensity. Tasting myself on his tongue was the last straw, and with a groan that disappeared into his mouth, I came all over his hand and my stomach.

The orgasm seemed to go on and on, and Daddy kissed me through it all, his tongue tasting each and every corner of my mouth as I did the same to him. It took me a good five minutes to get my breathing back under control, and he kept running his fingers through my short hair and down my cheek as he waited for me to catch my breath.

"That was . . ." I trailed off because I didn't have words for what that had been like. It had felt heavenly, but more than that, it had been so fucking beautiful. Sharing this with my daddy, it had been like a dream. And I couldn't wait to do more of it. The realization that I would have Daddy for the rest of my—apparently very long—life struck again, and I leaned up, puckering my lips for another kiss. Daddy pressed his lips to mine without a thought, giving me a sweet, gentle kiss. The kiss was very different than the one we had shared just moments ago, but no less special. This kiss was sweet and full of love and care. I wanted more of it. I wanted more of him.

When we were both breathless once again, Daddy pulled away and looked at me with his eyes full of love. I couldn't believe all that love was for me. Me, who had thought I would never find a daddy who would love me for who I was. I'd always expected to live alone or to be stuck in a relationship where I wouldn't be able to be who I truly was. And yet, here I was, making sweet, sweet love to my daddy who wanted me just the way I was. How did I get so lucky?

Birch

Westley looked absolutely sinful beneath me. His lips were still swollen red from our many kisses, his round cheeks flushed with arousal, and his stomach was covered in the cum I'd just wrung out of him. He looked dirty and debauched and all mine. I couldn't wait to claim him, to make him mine forever. But I also didn't want to rush straight to it. I wanted to savor this moment. After all, I would only get to claim him once.

And I wanted this to be a night he remembered for all of eternity.

"That was beautiful." I finished what he'd been about to say before trailing off, and he gave me a wide smile, nodding in agreement.

"You were so good, sweetheart. The way you gave yourself up to me, let me take care of you, it was beautiful. But we have the whole night ahead of us, remember? And here are some rules for what happens next. After this, you're not allowed to cum unless I say so. Understand?"

Westley nodded furiously, and I knew he would be a good boy. I'd been with a few brats before, but it was clear Westley wasn't one of them. Westley liked being a good boy, and I loved good boys. Scratch that. I loved Westley.

"All my orgasms are yours, Daddy." The way he said those words, with such an innocent and devoted look in his eyes, made my cock strain against my pants. I still hadn't removed them, and I liked having Westley spread out completely naked beneath me while I was still half dressed. But now, I needed more. Keeping my eyes on him, I pushed my pants down my thighs and slid out of them before dropping them off the bed. I grinned when Westley's eyes immediately jumped to my cock, and he swallowed hard, his hazel eyes darkening with need.

My cock was longer and slightly thinner than his, and I jacked myself slowly as my eyes roamed over Westley's smooth, gorgeous skin. The boy didn't realize how beautiful he was, but it was okay. I would show him. I would show him exactly how beautiful he was and make sure he never doubted his worth with me.

I kept pumping myself slowly as I took in the sweat-slicked skin of his neck and the beautiful arch that led down his chest toward his pretty pink nipples that stood all perked up, waiting for me to taste them.

A drop of precum oozed from the tip of my cock, and I wiped it off on my finger before offering it to Westley. I watched as he wrapped his wet lips around my finger and sucked firmly, showing me exactly how good he'd be if I stuck my cock into his mouth. I groaned low in my throat as he pulled my finger deeper into his mouth, slicking it with his saliva. Then he ran his tongue over the tip again and again. The feeling of his warm tongue on my finger shot an electric current straight to my cock, causing it to jump and leak steadily.

I pulled my finger away and claimed his lips with my own, moaning when I caught the faint taste of my precum on his tongue. I rubbed my spit-slicked finger over his hole, just firmly enough to drive him crazy. Westley shuddered beneath me, pushing down on my finger. I pulled my finger away, and he whined into my mouth but never stopped kissing me. I placed my finger on his hole once again, rubbing until he started pushing back and then I pulled away.

When I finally broke the kiss and sat back on my haunches, he was a mess. A beautiful mess that was all mine. His cock was hard and leaking as it rested on his stomach, his breathing harsh as he tried to get it under control. I'd planned on dragging this out a lot longer, until he was begging me to fuck him, but I didn't have the patience. I wanted to claim my boy now. I wanted to make him mine forever.

And anyway, I'd have the rest of our lives to tease him and play with him all I wanted to, wouldn't I?

"Do you have lube somewhere around here, Westley?" I asked and it seemed to take him a moment to process my question before he nodded and waved at the small bedside table. I pulled open the drawer and chuckled when I found the strawberry flavored lube. I made a note to remember my boy's preference as I grabbed the bottle that shared space with what looked like close to a hundred pins and badges. My boy sure had a collection.

"I can't pass you any diseases or get any from you, so we don't need a condom," I told him as I flicked the bottle open and breathed in the faint, sweet scent of strawberry. It was actually kind of . . . nice. Not too sharp a scent like I was expecting, but just enough to tickle my senses.

I slid down the bed, dropping kisses on my boy as I went. I took a moment to play with his pink nubs and only let up once I could feel he was close to the edge. I wanted him to cum with me inside him.

As I reached my destination, I licked my lips, my eyes roaming over my boy's full ass and his sweet hole. I grabbed his legs, kissing the sides of his knees as I urged him to spread them. Westley planted his feet away from his body, spreading his legs so I could see his hole better. I moaned at the beautiful sight and looked up at him. "You're gorgeous, my boy. So absolutely enchanting."

Westley flushed deep red, but he had a pleased smile on his face as he spread his legs further apart. I poured some lube onto my fingers before rubbing them over his hole. Just like before, I didn't slip my finger inside, just rubbed the edges of his hole until he was all loose and pliant for me.

I shifted, laying on my front so my face was between his legs and so very close to his hole. I breathed in the musky scent of his arousal, mixed in with the tang of sweat and the faint scent of strawberry, and my dick jerked as I moaned softly.

Unable to wait anymore, I ran my tongue around his hole, strawberry bursting across my tongue as I tasted the lube. It didn't taste bad, in any sense, but I wanted to taste my boy more. I plunged my tongue deeper into his hole and Westley moaned loudly, his hips jerking as he tried to keep himself from pushing down on me. He knew what would happen if he did that, and it was clear he didn't want me to stop.

I thrusted my tongue in and out of his hole, slow at first and then picking up the pace once he started loosening around me.

"More, Daddy! Please, more!" Westley begged, his voice breaking as he shuddered. And how could I deny my boy when he begged so beautifully to me?

I pulled away from him and he whined again, his eyes fluttering open. Before he could speak up, I poured more lube on my fingers and pressed two of them to his hole, raising a brow at him. He nodded instantly, but didn't push against my fingers. I smiled at him, at the way he so easily obeyed my command and pushed my fingers into him.

He groaned as I passed the tight ring of muscles. It was a snug fit, and I knew he must be feeling the burn, but judging from his expression, he liked it. I pumped my fingers, setting up a steady pace as Westley relaxed once again, his moans and groans filling the air.

After a while, I added another finger, thrusting into him faster and faster. I wanted to fuck him so badly, but I also didn't want to hurt him.

"Daddy, please. I want you. Fuck me, please."

At his groaned words, I pulled my fingers away and replaced them with my cock, pushing into him in one smooth thrust. I groaned as I bottomed out, my eyes fluttering shut as the wet heat of his channel surrounded me. God, he felt so good.

I started moving, pulling back—almost all the way out—before plunging into him. We both groaned as I bottomed out again and pressed against his prostate. I grabbed his ass with my palms, squeezing the ample flesh as I pulled him closer to me, his ass resting on my thighs as I pressed into him. I kissed any and every part of him that I could reach as my orgasm drew closer.

Westley's fingers were clutched tightly into the sheets, his teeth biting down on his lower lip so hard I feared he'd make it bleed. He was more gorgeous than anyone or anything I'd ever seen, and I felt so lucky to know that he was mine.

I grunted as my orgasm rushed up, the faint tingle of my magic following in its wake, and I met my boy's wide hazel eyes. "Cum for me, my sweet boy. Come for Daddy."

We came almost instantly, following each other over the edge as our orgasms burst through us. I slumped over him as my magic tingled in the background, binding me to this beautiful man, this boy who was everything I'd ever wanted, for all of eternity.

Westley's legs wrapped around my back, and we stayed like that for a few minutes before I could bring myself to pull away. I slid out of him slowly and he winced, but the expression on his face was anything but pain-filled. He looked sated, with a blissful smile on his face as he looked at me. I crawled up the bed until I was nose to nose with him before claiming his lips in a soft, gentle kiss. His lips were warm and wet and perfect against mine, and my dick gave a valiant effort as it tried to get hard again.

"Let me clean you up," I whispered against his lips as I moved to sit up, and his hand clutched my arm tightly, pulling my gaze back to him.

"Don't go, please."

"Just getting my shirt from the floor, baby. I'm not going anywhere, I promise."

Westley nodded and watched me intently as I leaned over the bed and grabbed my shirt from the floor. I wiped the lube from my hands before crawling over to Westley and wiping the mix of cum and lube from his ass, being careful around his hole. The cum on his stomach had dried already, so we'd need to shower to get rid of that, but it could wait. First, I wanted to cuddle with my boy for a bit.

I threw the shirt back from where I'd grabbed it from and lay down beside my boy, pulling him into my arms. He sighed softly, his arms tightening around me as he rested his head against my chest. We lay like that for a while, just enjoying our newly formed bond.

"I just realized something," Westley spoke up after a while and I jerked awake. I hadn't even realized I'd been drifting away, but my boy was pretty cozy company.

"What did you realize, Little Bunny?"

"That day on our date. In the park. When I wanted to play on the swings, and you said no one would notice. You used some kind of magic, didn't you? That's why no one pointed out how weird I was for playing on the swings like a kid."

"Hey, we talked about this. You're not weird."

"I know. I just meant that they didn't think it was weird because they—they couldn't see me, right?"

I smiled as I ran my fingers down his cheek, my thumb rubbing against his swollen lip. "That's right, Little Bunny. I used a bit of magic to make them look away."

"That's so cool," Westley murmured and I foresaw a really excited little asking me a million questions about my magic in the near future. I couldn't wait.

Westley's fingers scratched through my beard. He smiled at me, and his eyes were full of love as he said softly, "My Elf Daddy."

I smiled, my soul settling beside my other half's. "My Little Bunny."

Epilogue

Six Months Later

Birch

I paced in the living room as I waited for Westley to get here. After six months of dating, Westley was finally moving in with me. Honestly, I'd wanted him to move in with me the day I bought this house, but he'd said no. I couldn't fault him for it. Our romance had been kind of a whirlwind, and even though I'd claimed him within weeks of knowing him, there had been still a lot we hadn't known about each other. Westley had wanted to take it slow, and how could I say no to anything he wanted?

Which was why I'd spent the last six months getting to know my boy even better. I hadn't realized how much I still didn't know about him until we'd spent all that time together. And I was glad he'd told me no. I was glad we had taken the time to get to know each other before moving onto this next step. But I was equally excited to finally have him home with me, right where he belonged.

It wasn't like we had spent all that much time away from each other, anyway. Most days, I'd ended up sleeping at his cabin. But still, now he would be here with me all the time, sleep in my bed every night, and I couldn't wait. I'd wanted to go and pick him up myself, but Devon had insisted that he would drop him here. Westley didn't have a lot of belongings, and Devon had insisted that it would all fit in the truck, and therefore, he would be the one to drop Westley here. He was Westley's best friend, so I hadn't minded much, figuring it was something Devon wanted to do for his friend. I'd helped Westley pack yesterday, and seeing his meager possessions, I'd promised myself that I would give him the whole world and everything he desired. My boy deserved everything he wanted, and I was going to make sure he never lacked for anything.

The sound of tires against gravel pulled me out of my pacing, and I rushed over to the front door, flinging it open as the truck came to a stop in my driveway. I hurried over to the passenger side and opened Westley's door as soon as the truck had shut down. Westley smiled up at me, a wide grin that made his tiny dimples pop-up. That was another thing I hadn't noticed before, how adorable his dimples were. They rarely popped up, but when they did, they made his face look a hundred times brighter.

"You're here," I said softly as Westley got out of the truck and wrapped his arms around me. You'd think it had been months since we'd last seen each other with the way we were acting, but it was difficult to stay away from your Fated one. I'd learned it the hard way, and I was glad I wouldn't have to stay away from him anymore.

Devon got out of the truck and shook his head at us, his long braid whipping around. "Oh, I see how it is. I'm just the chauffeur now, aren't I?"

Westley flushed as he pulled away from me and turned to look at Devon, shaking his head instantly.

"Oh no, Dev. I'm sorry," Westley hurried to say, but Devon's smirk stopped him before he could keep apologizing.

"It's okay, Westley. I was just teasing you. Now, let's get your stuff out of the truck." Devon walked to the bed and heaved two of Westley's bags out, holding one in each hand and carting them inside. Westley shook his head before heading over to grab a box. I followed his lead, grabbing boxes and carrying them inside. Within minutes, we had everything moved into the living room, and I smiled as I saw Westley's stuff among mine. Finally, my boy was where he was supposed to be.

"Would you like to stay for some time, Devon?" Westley asked, and though I wanted nothing more than to spend some time with him, just him, I couldn't fault him for asking after all the help Devon had given us. Plus, this was his home too now, and he had every right to invite his friends over.

Devon shook his head, eyeing me with a knowing glint in his eyes before he turned to Westley. "Oh no, I can't stay. I have the day off, so I'm going to help Rebba out with some things since Caleb is taking Noel on a date and she'll be short-staffed. I'll leave you be so you can start christening your new house. I bet your daddy has some plans for you." Devon winked at Westley, who flushed red and shook his head. Devon walked closer to us and pulled Westley into a hug, something that seemed to surprise Westley, judging by the squeaky sound he made.

When Devon pulled away, he had an unreadable look on his face. He turned toward me, leaned closer, and took a deep breath. His eyes widened, and his gaze shot up to me. "Where did you go today? Before we got here?"

I shot Westley a glance, but he seemed as puzzled about Devon's question as I was. I could see that the question was important to him, though, so I told him. "Um, I visited The Happy Place this morning. Rebba was holding a . . . package for me." It was a surprise for Westley, something he'd see in a few minutes, but I didn't want to explain further, and I hoped Devon wouldn't ask.

Wes shot me a curious look, and I knew he was wondering why I'd gone to the pet shelter Rebba ran, but he'd find out soon enough. Devon, on the other hand, looked ready to bolt. "Is everything okay, Devon?"

He nodded distractedly as he pulled his phone out of his pocket before nodding at Westley. "I'll see you around, okay?"

He had his phone pressed to his ear as he turned around, and then he was hurrying out the door. "Hey, Rebba. Is anyone in right now? What about . . ." His voice drifted off before I heard the truck door slam shut, and with the roaring sound of the engine, he was gone.

I turned to look at Westley. "Any idea what that was about?" He shook his head, shrugging, and I noticed that his cheeks were still pink from his earlier blush. After a few weeks of dating, Westley had admitted the nature of our relationship to his friends. I'd told him he didn't have to if he didn't want to, but he'd insisted on it. He hadn't liked keeping it a secret, and I was glad his friends had taken it well. Gus—the ray of sunshine that was now our neighbor a few houses over—had been especially ecstatic. He'd been studying gender and sexuality, he'd told us, since he'd missed so many of the changes that had taken place in the past century and a half while he'd been stuck in a vampire sleep, and he'd assured Westley that he understood him completely and wouldn't mind having a playdate with him as a big brother someday, either.

I chuckled at the blush that covered my boy's cheeks before pulling him into my arms and pressing a kiss on top of his head. "Come on, I want to show you something." I led him down the hallway to a closed room but stopped before I opened it.

Turning to him, I pulled out the blindfold I had stashed in my pocket earlier and offered it to him. He stared at it with wide eyes before looking up at me.

"I don't know how I feel about using a blindfold." His cheeks flushed darker, and I chuckled as I realized what he was thinking.

"Don't worry, we're not doing anything kinky. Unless you want to," I added with a wink.

Westley blushed furiously, and I chuckled as I placed the blindfold around his eyes, adjusting it so he wouldn't be able to see around it.

"Are you ready?"

"I guess?" Westley asked and I grinned as I imagined his reaction to what I was about to show him.

I opened the door and led him in, then closed the door behind me. Once he was in the middle of the room, I pulled the blindfold off him and told him to open his eyes.

His eyes fluttered open slowly, and he blinked a few times before his eyes took in everything. The walls were painted in pastel colors: lavender on one wall, pink on the other, blue on the third, and green on the fourth. One side of the room was covered with shelves that had toys of all kinds for my little bunny. Another wall had shelves full of stuffed toys, since they were my boy's favorites. There was a small closet beside the shelf with the stuffed toys which held all of his play clothes. A large mat was spread across the room so my boy could play anywhere he wanted without hurting his knees. But the thing that had captured my boy's attention almost instantly was against the far corner of the room.

The big playpen housed three bunnies. The same three bunnies I had found Westley playing with all those months ago, when I'd discovered that he was, in fact, a little. Rebba had been holding them at the shelter for me, and I'd picked them up earlier today. Westley was surprised because they'd told him the three bunnies had been adopted, which had crushed my sweet boy. I'd almost broken down and admitted I had them, but the thought of getting to see this exact look of delight on his face had helped me hold onto the secret.

Westley gasped as he took in the bunnies, turning to look at me with wide eyes. "You adopted Snuggles, Sleepy, and Cookie? For me? Really? I get to keep them?" The questions followed one after the other in usual Westley fashion, and I grinned at his excitement.

"They're all yours, baby. I know how much you love them, and I know you wanted to adopt them."

"I never thought . . . I never thought I'd be able to, what with how much I had to work and the fact that I didn't have . . . well, I didn't have enough money to take care of them properly. But I can keep them? Really?"

"Really. They are a gift from me to you. Now, what do you think about the rest of the room?" I held my breath as I waited for his reply, but he surprised me by throwing his arms around me and hugging me tightly. I held him to me, asking softly as he clung to me, "Westley? You okay?"

He nodded against my shoulder but still didn't move, so I held him to me as I waited for him to gather his thoughts. After a few minutes, Westley pulled away and smiled at me, his eyes full of love for me.

"I love you, Daddy. You have given so much to me. I don't just mean material things like these, even though I absolutely love this room and can't wait to play in it. You've given me so much more than that. You have shown me that I am perfect just the way I am, that the things I thought made me weird are some of the best things about me. You have shown me that the size of my body doesn't matter when it comes to what I want and who I am. You've shown me that I can be a *little* and big at the same time. You have accepted me just the way I am, and I love you for it. Thank you for being my daddy."

He pulled something out of his pocket and offered it to me, and I glanced down at the badge he held in his palm. It was clear he'd had it specially made for me, and I took it from him and turned it around so I could read what it said. *Little Bunny's Daddy*, the badge read, and I smiled as I pinned it on my shirt before looking up at him again. He had a wide smile on his face as he looked at the badge on my chest, and I knew I would treasure this little token forever.

I blinked away the moisture in my eyes and wrapped my arms around Westley, pulling him into a hug this time. I squeezed him tightly once before pulling back and claiming his lips. I kissed him reverently, showing him just how much I loved him, how much he meant to me. He said I'd shown him how perfect he was, but he had done the same for me. He'd shown me that being a daddy didn't require me to be a certain way. Just like he wasn't a typical little, I wasn't the typical daddy, but that didn't matter when your heart wanted what it wanted. And mine wanted Westley, for now and ever.

I pulled away after a minute, resting my forehead against his. "How about we play here for a bit, and then we can think about that christening Devon mentioned?" I offered and Westley flushed red before pulling back and raising a brow at me.

"How about we take care of the christening first and then come here to play?" Westley asked, his cheeks flaming brighter even as he stood firm, and I fell just a little bit more in love with him.

*Want more of Westley and Birch? Read a
bonus scene
by subscribing to Stella's newsletter!*

Curious about Devon? Read his story in Claws, available on Kindle Unlimited!

Also By Stella

PARANORMAL ROMANCE

Set in Mistvale

Mages of Ravenshire:
Set in the fictional town of Mistvale, Mages of Ravenshire is a series filled with magic, laughs and love. Low on angst and high on sweetness, Mages of Ravenshire will leave you with a smile on your face. Come meet Neya, Pads, April, and all the other fur-babies and their humans, vampires and mages.

Touch of Magic. (Goofy mage x nerdy human)

Sleep of Eternity. (Grumpy mage x sunshine vampire)

Angel of Death. (Sweet necromancer x snarky vampire)

Boxset. (With a special bonus scene.)

Misfits of Mistvale:
With side-characters from Mages of Ravenshire, this series features shifters, half-mermen, werewolves, and many more supernaturals. With the usual dose of fur-babies, found family, and all the Mistvale feels, this series features standalones with a different couple in each book.

Claws. (Graysexual bobcat x cat shifter)

Tails. (Merman-siren x dolphin shifter)

Bonds. (Human x femme wolf shifter x asexual werewolf)

Mistvale Spin-Off Novellas:
Featuring various side-characters from the town of Mistvale, these novellas are full of sweet, fuzzy romance, and the meddlesome cast of Mistvale.

My Elf Mate. (GFY, holiday, elf x wolf shifter.)

<u>My Dragon Mate</u>. (Bi-awakening, human x dragon.)

<u>My Elf Daddy</u>. (Daddy/little, elf x human.)

<u>My Fae Mate</u>. (Genderfluid MC, holiday, Fate x Alchemist.)

<u>Make A Wish</u>. (Djinn x Human, free read.)

Set in Otherworld

Fate's Gambit Trilogy:
Fate's Gambit is an MMM PNR trilogy featuring a sweet, subby cinnamon-bun devil, a gentle-giant who's a service sub/Daddy switch, and a slightly frustrated Master as they slowly figure our their dynamic and fall madly in love. They're joined by annoyingly awesome side-characters including a sweet hedgehog, a sassy talking snake, and a guardian in the form of a cat-man. This trilogy features the same triad and needs to be read in order.

<u>First Play</u>. (Free Prequel.)

<u>Devil's Gamble</u>.

<u>Pet's Ploy</u>.

<u>Master's Design</u>.

<u>Boxset</u>.

Lords of Otherworld:
Following the events of Fate's Gambit, Lords of Otherworld delves deeper into the workings of Otherworld, with new characters, new romance, and new adventures. With found family vibes, danger and romance, each book in this series follows a different couple, with an overarching storyline. It is recommended to read the books in order.

<u>Maximus</u>.

<u>Zane</u>.

<u>Nox</u>.

Standalones

<u>Elijah Summons A Demon</u> (A newsletter serial.)

CONTEMPORARY ROMANCE

Voice Out

<u>Weathering The Storm</u> (Roommates to lovers, hurt/comfort.)

<u>Watching The Sunrise</u> (Friends to lovers, genderfluid MC.)

About Stella

Stella Rainbow lives in a small town in India with her family and her five-year-old cat, Harry, who is her number one supporter, cuddle buddy, and writing buddy all rolled into one.

Living with a chronic illness, Stella grew up with books as her best friends, and now she writes in the hopes of giving others like her a reprieve from the real world.

Stella's books are low on the angst, high on the sweetness, with a doze of found family, and some absolutely adorable fur—and sometimes scale—babies.

You can join her mailing list to receive updates about her books and free content. You can also read more about Stella, her books, and the universe she writes in on her website, www.authorstellarainbow.com.

You can also follow her on:

Facebook: Stella Rainbow
Instagram: @authorstellarainbow

Goodreads: Stella Rainbow
BookBub: Stella Rainbow
Amazon: Stella Rainbow

www.ingramcontent.com/pod-product-compliance
Lightning Source LLC
Chambersburg PA
CBHW051221160726
47994CB00002B/695